# ACCLAIM FOR
# MARCIA MULLER AND

## *CITY OF WHISPERS*

"McCone is the new breed of American woman detective...redefining the mystery genre by applying different sensibilities and values to it."

*—New York Times Book Review*

"Enjoyable...It'll certainly keep you entertained."

*—Charleston Post and Courier* (SC)

"A gripping mystery...crisp dialogue, great plot, and the sharp and savvy detective make this one of the best reads of the year."

*—Toronto Saturday Star*

"The narrative shifts perspective among several of the main players...lending the novel an overview not always possible when writing strictly in the first person. Marcia Muller, a recipient of the Mystery Writers of America Grand Master Award, is up to the task. And hey, if you like this story, there are 28 additional McCone novels in this long-running series!"

*—BookPage*

"Sharon McCone is one of the most interesting fictional private detectives in the genre today...there is never a dull moment during one of her cases...The final chapters are full of action and will keep you guessing until the end."

—BookReporter.com

"One of the treasures of the genre."

—*Chicago Tribune*

"Alternating chapters narrated by different characters add to the suspense of the intricate plot, which propels readers through a San Francisco few tourists see—from Colma, the city's necropolis, to the exclusive mansions of Sea Cliff—and to a harrowing, haunting denouement."

—*Publishers Weekly*

"One of the world's premier mystery writers."

—*Cleveland Plain Dealer*

"Ms. Muller's plotting is masterful, with her sure-footed, economical storytelling—even with the changes of narrator from chapter to chapter—supporting the plot as it glides easily along. And that takes some great writing."

—*New York Journal of Books*

"Her stories crackle like few others on the mystery landscape."

—*San Francisco Examiner & Chronicle*

# CITY OF WHISPERS

# CITY OF WHISPERS

## MARCIA MULLER

**GRAND CENTRAL**
**PUBLISHING**

NEW YORK    BOSTON

Copyright © 2011 by Pronzini-Muller Family Trust
Excerpt from *Looking for Yesterday* copyright © 2012 by Pronzini-Muller Family Trust

Grand Central Publishing
Hachette Book Group
237 Park Avenue
New York, NY 10017
www.HachetteBookGroup.com

Grand Central Publishing is a division of Hachette Book Group, Inc.
The Grand Central Publishing name and logo is a trademark of Hachette Book Group, Inc.

The Hachette Speakers Bureau provides a wide range of authors for speaking events. To find out more, go to www.hachettespeakersbureau.com or call (866) 376-6591.

The publisher is not responsible for websites (or their content) that are not owned by the publisher.

Printed in the United States of America

Originally published in hardcover by Hachette Book Group
First mass market edition: September 2012

10  9  8  7  6  5  4  3  2  1
OPM

For Marcie Galick

Special thanks to Bill,
for his suggestions, time, and support.

# CITY OF WHISPERS

# Sharon McCone

Sometimes when I'm alone and can't sleep I listen to the sounds of the city.

The grinding and clanging of the J-Church streetcar as it rounds the turn and stops on Thirtieth Street. Foghorns moaning out at the Golden Gate. Cars rumbling, dogs howling, the neighbors' TVs mumbling. The occasional conversations of passersby and the white noise of the freeways.

But mostly what I listen to is whispers.

*This city, it makes me afraid.*

*I love you....*

*Nobody can find out what I did.*

*Out here nobody looks at me.*

*What happened to you?*

*The night is different.*

*How could you do this to me?*

*I love you....*
*I couldn't've done that....*
*Tell me everything about that time.*
*I hurt all over.*
*Dark, like it's supposed to be when you're dead.*
*Where am I?*
*Maybe I'm dead.*

Of course the whispers are echoes of my past. I've heard them all over time. But I suspect that somewhere in the city these words, or very similar ones, are still being spoken.

This city is large and diverse. There are pockets of grinding poverty, pockets of middle-class respectability, pockets of wealth. There is corruption beyond a normal person's belief, and incredible selflessness and valor. Intrigue worthy of a spy novel, and innocence and wonder. Eight hundred thousand–plus people, living out their stories.

And all too often, their stories merge with mine.

# TUESDAY, SEPTEMBER 7

# Sharon McCone

September in the city, Labor Day barbecues in a misty fog come and gone. On this day, glorious sunshine and clear blue skies. Our summer was about to begin.

I climbed the stairway to the agency's offices off the north-side catwalk of Pier 24½. Waved to everybody as I passed their open doors. Flopped my briefcase on my desk, sat down, and opened my e-mail.

Reports on cases from my nephew and techno-whiz Mick Savage. Copies of correspondence from the other operatives. A plaintive note from Ma: "When are you going to forgive me?"

For what? Because she'd gone ballistic after I'd been shot in the head and trapped for a time in a locked-in state? (Like a coma, except I was aware of everything around me, could hear and see but not move or communicate except for eyeblinks. Believe me, that is one of the lower levels of hell.) And when your mother hurls herself on your chest, weeping and wailing, it only makes the situation worse.

My hospitalization had ended a year ago; I'd gone through intensive physical therapy and still worked out several times a week at a gym. Occasionally I tired easily and there were periods when—asleep or awake—I'd flash back to the shooting and experience drenching sweats, shakiness, and disorientation. But basically I was okay and improving steadily. Eventually, my neurologist told me, the aftereffects would disappear. I wasn't so sure of that, but they were things I was learning to live with.

This message from Ma—her stock in trade is histrionics and she wouldn't be Ma without them. Likely she, recently widowed and a new convert to e-mail, had written this to one of my three siblings and sent it to the wrong address. And what would she be asking any of them to forgive her for? I'd have to check with them.

My other mother, the one who had given birth to me and put me up for adoption, had forwarded a notice of her upcoming appearance on *Good Morning America*. Saskia Blackhawk was a Boise, Idaho, attorney who had argued Indian-rights cases all the way to the Supreme Court—and won every time. She was much sought after on the talk-show circuit.

Nothing from Hy, currently in Zurich, on a case involving the changing privacy rules of the Swiss banks. Nothing from my friend Piper, who had promised to look into memberships for us in the Academy of Sciences in Golden Gate Park.

A notice from the city port commission about a scheduled hearing on demolishing old piers. Pier 24½ was in that category, in spite of the thriving businesses that rented space here. So far, with the intervention of a powerful attorney friend of mine, we had been spared. But for how much longer?

I put the thought aside and opened the rest of my mail. Client, commending me for a job well done. Humane Society, thanking me for my contribution. Democrats.org: breaking news, not good. Coldwater Creek: my order had shipped.

Again from sblackhawk@comcast.net, only the subject line read, "From Darcy." The message was brief: "Help me. I'm in SF."

He was piggybacking off Saskia's account. Probably had stolen her password; she never would have given it to him.

Bet he wanted money.

Darcy Blackhawk was my half brother from Saskia's long marriage to Thomas Blackhawk, a fellow attorney who had died several years ago. They'd also had a daughter, Robin, currently enrolled in law school at Berkeley's Boalt Hall. Unlike his sister, Darcy was a troubled kid who'd dropped out of school, done a wide assortment of drugs, and run with bad companions, and who couldn't hold down a job for more than a week. He'd briefly turned his life around, about the time I discovered my other family, and gotten a job editing videos for a local TV station. But the desire for drugs had proven stronger than the desire for success, and while stoned he'd destroyed the footage of a violent antiabortion demonstration during which a woman was fatally shot. He'd been fired, then had backslid and sunk to a new low.

Saskia couldn't keep track of him, although periodically he turned up at her house for food or shelter. Last she'd heard he'd been living under a bridge on the Middle Fork of the Salmon River, northeast of Boise near Challis. In a recent phone conversation Saskia had said bitterly, "Ironic that it's also called the River of No Return."

And I had thought, *Under a bridge just like a troll.*

Well, the troll was on the move. No computers under bridges—usually.

I shot the message over to Mick, asking him if he could find out where it was sent from—probably some Internet café. Not an easy task for most people to accomplish quickly, but a snap for the co-creator of SavageFor.com, a real-time search engine under the management of the giant Omnivore. Mick knew the side roads and back alleys of the Internet, and could get from one to another in his sleep.

Then I carefully composed a reply to Darcy.

Of course I'll help you, but I need more information. Where are you? And what's the problem? You know you can always come to me, either at the pier or at home. I miss you and love you. —S

I looked critically at what I'd written, then deleted the last sentence. Neither sentiment was true.

Next I called Saskia in Boise.

"You're about to get a strange message from me," I told her. "Darcy's using your Comcast account from someplace here in San Francisco. He sent me a message asking for help. I replied to him, hoping he'll tap into your mail again."

"That little—" She broke off, but it was obvious what the next word would've been. "How did he get my password?"

"How does he get anything?"

"Steals. Sometimes I let myself forget that he's not stupid, just emotionally challenged."

Darcy was expert at taking money from a till when a cashier had his or her back turned; he'd never held up anyplace—as far as anyone knew—but he'd cadged large amounts from people on the street who felt sorry for him or were afraid of his craziness.

"How long d'you suppose he's been down here?" I asked. "He was still on the Salmon River a month ago."

"I don't know. What does he want you to help him with?"

"He didn't say. Money, probably. I'm assuming he'll get back to me. Do you know any reason for him to come to the Bay Area?"

"...No. Robin's made it clear she doesn't want to see him, and I think she's warned him not to bother you."

Robin and Darcy couldn't be more different. Robin's feelings for her brother were complex: compassion because he was a weak and troubled man; anger because he'd taken advantage of her one time too many; a strong desire to keep him out of her life; an equally strong desire to protect her mother from him. And, I supposed, a little bit of love because he was, after all, her brother.

"Has he been in any trouble recently?" I asked.

"Only the usual." Saskia's tone was wry with a touch of sadness.

"What's 'the usual'?"

"Shoplifting. He tried to steal a whole ham from the supermarket. Do you know what kind of bulge a whole ham makes under a hoodie? And then it turned out the hoodie still had its tags on it—he'd taken it from Kmart the day before."

Uh-huh. Maybe Darce *was* stupid.

"Anything else?"

"Oh, items have disappeared from my house: cash, soap, towels, one of his father's golfing trophies that could easily be pawned. Cereal, his favorite kind, Froot Loops."

*How appropriate.*

"There's something else too," Saskia added. "He assaulted a police officer."

"Great. When, where, and why?"

"About ten days ago. Under the bridge on the Salmon River. The police were removing him and the other homeless persons from their encampment—that's how I knew he was there."

"You bail him out?"

"Yes."

"And he took off."

"Well, he came home for a few hours. Then, according to my neighbor, a woman—a druggie friend, no doubt— appeared, and the two of them left with my silver tea set."

Saskia's voice, usually so forceful and assured, was clogged with shame and grief. "Sharon," she added, "I think he's getting worse."

"In what ways?"

"At times he can pass for lucid, but mostly he slips in and out of reality. Sometimes you look into his eyes and wonder if he's really all there. I'm surprised he remembered your e-mail address, but sometimes bits of factual information pop into his mind, and he uses them. Other times—" She broke off, her voice ragged.

I spared her any more questioning, simply saying, "I'll find out what he's up to and keep you posted."

As I waited for Mick to get back to me I thought about my birth family. A few years ago, when the father who had raised me died, he'd left me the task of disposing of the contents of his garage—no small chore, since no McCone had ever thrown anything out. The Pack Rat Family. There, in a carton of personal papers, I found—as Pa had intended me to—my adoption papers.

Ma refused to talk about them. My siblings didn't know anything, had always believed we were blood relatives, even though my dark Indian looks had contrasted markedly with their blond Scotch-Irish appearance. I was a throwback to my Shoshone great-grandmother, my parents had told us. Nobody'd questioned that; it's a scientific fact that throwbacks do exist.

So after finding the document I'd begun a search for my birth parents. Who else was so suited to the task? It eventually led me to the Flathead Reservation in Montana, where I found my father, a Shoshone artist named Elwood Farmer, who had married a Flathead woman and moved there many years ago. Then I traced Saskia to Boise, Idaho. Elwood and I were still struggling toward defining our relationship, but Saskia and Robin and I had become a family of sorts—with Darcy always lurking on the edges. He seemed to resent our closeness but made no effort to join in. Or maybe he *didn't* resent it, simply had no capacity to relate.

Either way, none of us could understand the tangles and turns of Darcy's mind, and if what Saskia said about his getting worse was true, those tangles and turns would be even more impenetrable now. He shouldn't be running free on the streets, where he was a danger to himself and others—

My cell rang. Ma. E-mail had failed her so she'd resorted to her favorite form of communication.

"Are you still mad at me?"

So the e-mail had been intended for me after all. "For what?"

"Well, I sent those new pink bedroom slippers I bought for you to Patsy and she kept them."

"Patsy has huge feet; they couldn't have fit her."

"They were stretchy."

"Ma—"

"I called her and asked her to send them to you, but she denies having received them."

"Probably she didn't."

"That's right. Just an hour ago I found a delivery confirmation receipt here. They went to John."

Not only was she confusing her three daughters, but all her children. I suppressed a laugh, imagining what John must have thought when he opened a package containing stretchy—and probably fuzzy—pink slippers.

"Tell John to send them to me." I spoke in a light tone, but I was really concerned. Pa had died years ago, and it had been a year and a half since Melvin Hunt, Ma's second husband, succumbed to cancer. Ma didn't know what to do with herself, and it was making her mentally lazy— something she'd never been.

"Oh, I'll do that," she said. "So you aren't mad at me?"

"Why would I be?"

"Well, one of my children is. I can feel it."

Ma had always been overly imaginative, so her response didn't surprise me, but it alarmed me a bit. However, now was not the time to suggest she get out more, become a charity volunteer, or take a course in ceramics at the senior center. I chatted a bit and ended the call.

An aging parent. I'd been warned about this. But Ma was healthy and had a lot of good years left. I didn't believe in interfering with what someone wanted to do with her life, yet I sensed she was reaching out. A family council meeting was in order soon.

Mick stood in the doorway—tall, blond, trim, and handsome. Even I considered him handsome, and I'd known him as a scowly, mean little brat not too many years ago.

"Darcy's message was sent from an Internet café on Chestnut Street," he said. "It's called The Wiring Hall."

"The Marina." It wasn't a neighborhood where I could picture Darcy. The district fronting the Bay east of the Golden Gate Bridge was distinctly upscale; nowhere in the city could you see more well-dressed mommies and daddies pushing expensive baby strollers and walking pedigreed dogs.

"Yep. You heard back from him yet?"

"No."

"Figures."

Even though Mick was himself a former fuckup, he didn't like Darcy. Well, neither did I, much.

Mick said, "Why did he e-mail you? He could've come here to the pier or your house."

"Darcy's brain is...wired differently than most people's. He has no sense of results or consequences. When the impulse strikes him, whatever he wants to happen has got to happen now, not later. He may have gone into the

café to get change so he could call me, but then he saw a
computer terminal. And there you have it."

"And everybody—you, Saskia, and Robin—just puts
up with this kind of behavior?"

"Pretty much. He's been in and out of psychiatric institutions, but none of them did any good."

"Seems to me you three should lose him."

That made sense, but both Mick and I knew from tough
experience that when someone who's related to you asks
for help, help is what you've got to give.

My intercom buzzed. Ted, our super-efficient office
manager—or, as he preferred to call himself, Grand
Poobah—said, "Mr. MacGruder is here."

MacGruder: a prospective client, potentially lucrative.
He owned a medium-sized software firm and was concerned about employee espionage.

I said to Mick, "Can you take over with this client?
MacGruder, I told you about him. I need to start looking
for Darcy."

"Shar, the important clients need to initially meet with
the head of the agency. That's what they expect, and what
we give."

"But Darcy—"

"I'll go look for him. You stay here and don't worry."

But I *would* worry. I didn't doubt Mick's abilities, but I
was a hands-on investigator. I'd worry plenty....

# Mick Savage

*This business with Darcy is going to be trouble*, he thought as he went back to his office. The guy was bad news and he pulled other people down.

Like the time after the wedding reception Grandma had thrown for Shar and Hy, when Darcy set the shrubbery behind her garage on fire while smoking dope. And the time he wrecked his sister Robin's apartment in Berkeley, bringing home three derelicts he'd met on Telegraph Avenue and leaving behind empty bottles, smashed glasses, cigarette-burned furniture, stained carpets, torn draperies, and a broken oven door—all of which was accomplished in one afternoon while she was in her torts class. He'd cost Saskia plenty for fines, bail, and settlements to ward off lawsuits.

And now this troll stuff...

Asshole *deserved* to live under a bridge.

Mick went into his office and slumped in his swivel chair. Derek Ford, the other member of McCone Investigations' geek squad, wasn't there, had probably gone out for coffee. After a moment's reflection Mick dialed Robbie Blackhawk's number in Berkeley. She picked up immediately, her crisp, hurried tone making her sound as if he'd caught her on her way out. "Has Darcy contacted you?" he asked.

"Who? Darcy? No."

"He's in the city, just e-mailed Shar wanting help."

"Help with what?"

"He didn't say."

"Shit." Her voice was flat.

"Did you change the locks after that time he trashed your place?"

"Yes. Dammit, what's he gotten himself into *this* time?"

"Whatever it is, it wouldn't surprise me. If you hear from him, give me a call. And don't tell Shar I got in touch with you."

"Right. Got to go."

Mick considered calling his girlfriend, Alison Lawton, then remembered she, a stockbroker with Merrill Lynch, had told him she had client meetings scheduled back-to-back for most of the day. Two careers, not much time, but when they were together…

He gathered up his jacket and keys, went down the stairs to the floor of the pier, and got on his Harley. Now that he thought about it, he regretted giving Shar the information about where Darcy had e-mailed from. He knew his aunt; even though he'd said he'd look for Darcy, she'd head to The Wiring Hall as soon as she was free and launch an all-out search for her half brother. If she found him—and she would, Mick was sure of that—she'd bring him home and try to rehabilitate him. It wouldn't work, of course, and she'd be heartbroken. Maybe then Darcy would take up residence under the Golden Gate Bridge—hopefully in the shipping lanes.

*Harsh, Savage. Harsh.*

He started the bike and headed for Chestnut Street.

Parking in the Marina district was impossible, as always, even with a motorcycle like his Harley. Finally he found a space three blocks from the café that he could wedge the bike into without fear of its being damaged by the vehicles to either side.

The Wiring Hall had neon tubes designed to look like lightning bolts in its large front windows. Inside it was all high-tech aluminum. Several people hunched over their laptops and lattes or used the terminals provided by the café, and none looked up when Mick strode to the counter. A woman of about his age with a tattoo of red rosebuds covering half her face was standing by the register, counting out dollar bills. She'd probably had the tat since her late teens, and Mick wondered if she now regretted it. She would someday, like as not, when the wrinkles set in and all those pretty flowers wilted. . . .

He ordered black coffee, and when the woman brought it, said, "Guy was in here maybe an hour and a half ago. Used one of your terminals. You'd have noticed him: Indian features, funny dyed hair, lots of piercings. Scruffy. Didn't fit the neighborhood."

"I'd've noticed him if I was on shift then, but mine just started."

"Who was on then?"

She eyed him suspiciously. He took out his ID case and handed it to her.

"Okay," she said, returning the case to him. "What are you after the guy for?"

"Nothing bad. He's just a missing person."

"Oh. Well, then, the person to talk to is Mira. Mira Rasmussen."

"Where can I find her?"

"Usually she has lunch at Zero's."

Mick knew Zero's. Small and narrow and noisy and way too expensive. Very popular and God knew why; the food was atrocious. An odd place for a coffee barista to frequently lunch, but then maybe she had odd taste. He walked the two blocks down Chestnut to Zero's and went inside. The long bar down the right-hand side was crowded. He shouldered between two suits and asked the barman for Mira Rasmussen.

"She's out back, having lunch."

"Out back?"

"Yeah—like in the kitchen."

"Why there?"

"She's the owner's old lady, works down the block." Someone at the other end of the bar was gesturing for service. "Go straight back through those swinging doors, and you'll find her."

Mick went past closely packed tables where people were eating sandwiches dripping with oddly colored veggie mixes, weird-looking salads, and pizzettas loaded with things like arugula and pineapple.

*Thank God for steak and fried chicken and meat lasagna!*

Behind the swinging doors the kitchen was hot and fragrant with the foods being prepared by a busy staff of five. At the far end of a central prep island, where a short Latino man was chopping tomatoes and onions, a woman with long, dusky hair and large tortoiseshell glasses sat reading the *Chronicle* and spooning up soup. The soup, Mick noted, was an odd yellow-green and had...things floating in it.

He went to her, introduced himself, and showed his ID.

She looked a little surprised—she'd probably never met a private investigator, and he was relatively young for the job—then held out her hand and said, "What can I do for you?"

He described Darcy, asked, "Did you see him?"

"How could I not? He came in during the early rush, went straight to use one of the terminals, and sent a quick message. A woman who came in after him tried to stop him from sending it, but too late. Then they left."

"Did you notice anything odd about him, other than his appearance?"

She considered. "He acted...well, furtive. And he kept glancing at the woman as if he were afraid of her. Also, he was whispering to himself."

"You hear what he whispered?"

"Only a phrase. 'The palace, the coral tree.' Weird, huh?"

"Yeah. This woman—can you describe her?"

"Long blond hair. Short. Shabby clothes. I didn't get a good look at her face."

"Anything else?" Mick asked.

"The guy grabbed a handful of straws from the condiment station on his way out."

"Straws?"

"Plastic straws for smoothies. Red-white-and-blue-striped."

"You see which way he went when he left?"

"West, toward Divisidero. The woman was hanging on to his arm."

"Thanks. If you remember anything else, you have my card." Mick started across the kitchen, then turned. "By the way, what color is his hair these days?"

"Greenish, an odd yellow-green."

Like the awful-looking soup she was eating with apparent relish.

# Darcy Blackhawk

*This city, it makes me afraid.*

Shouldn't, he knew. Wasn't like the movies he'd seen of New York, with its crowds and subways and taxicabs that nearly clipped you every time you crossed the street. Or LA—all those messed-up freeways. Or Seattle—that city he knew for real—where if your Indian blood showed on your face, they treated you like some drunken bum. He'd been worse places than San Francisco.

When, though?

And why *was* he here?

He was still drugged up from the cocaine he'd shared with Laura before. Now he shook his head, felt the first symptoms of vertigo, and heard a shushing sound in his ears. Leaned against a lamppost and peered up at the street sign: Lyon and California. How the hell had he gotten here? He was supposed to be someplace else. Some palace. Or maybe he'd already been there . . .

A woman said, "Darcy? You okay?"

He knew her, but he couldn't remember her name. In her twenties, maybe. Long, dirty, blond hair and gray eyes. Brown cape with fringe that hung almost to her ankles. Sandals and a silver toe ring. She'd come up to him like this before, when he'd found Laura. Laura, who had gone to meet her connection. Laura'd needed a fix bad after two months in jail.

"Darcy?"

He swayed, and the girl put an arm around his shoulders to steady him. She was very strong.

"Palace," he said. "Have to go to the palace."

"You're sick," she said.

"Have to go Gaby's grave."

"Gaby! Why?"

"Grave. Under a coral tree. Some . . . reason . . ."

"Something there?"

". . . Maybe."

"Let me help you."

He shivered and clung to her while she hailed a cab.

He didn't want to go with her, but Shar hadn't answered his e-mail. No wonder—he didn't have his laptop any more—he'd sold that a long time ago. But didn't Shar know he had e-mail in his head?

Or did he? Nobody had sent him a message in . . . what? Months?

A cab pulled to the curb. Yellow. Were they all yellow in San Francisco? Or was that someplace else? The girl helped him in, leaned forward, and whispered an address to the driver.

He took out one of the drinking straws he'd gotten at the café. Twisted it, released it, twisted it again. An old habit, twisting things; it helped him focus.

Not now, though: the vertigo got worse and bile was rising in his throat. He forced it down, dropped the straw, pressed his face into the scratchy wool of the girl's cape.

*This city, it makes me afraid....*

# Sharon McCone

The last of my new clients left my office, bound for an interview with Julia Rafael, the operative to whom I'd assigned his case. The others had said they would let me know if they required our services, meaning the fee had put them off. But this latest, a businessman asking for a fairly routine skip trace on a former employee, had wanted to get started immediately.

When I swiveled around I was looking through the big arched window behind my desk. Beyond it the Bay sparkled, the bridge spanning it and disappearing into the tunnel on Treasure Island. Sailboats glided over the blue water. I loved these offices in the pier, but there had been those rumblings from City Hall about demolishing it. If that happened I'd have to move the agency. But where? Not one of the bland office towers that were springing up like mushrooms all over the area. Maybe one of the outlying neighborhoods? Someplace with cheaper rents and more plentiful parking?

No, I didn't like that idea. The kind of clients we were now attracting expected upscale offices. Ours here certainly weren't luxurious, but our being in a pier had a certain cachet that made them take little notice of the décor. We'd been doing so well recently that I'd hoped to put the surplus profits into employee raises and health-care options. This impending move would put those plans on hold.

I should have been dealing with the rental-space problem, but I had a more immediate one: Darcy. I'd promised Saskia I'd find him, then had let Mick take over for me, and now I'd heard nothing from Mick.

I checked my phone to see if there was a message from him on voice mail. Nothing. I called his cell, but apparently he'd turned it off. Damn! Of course, Mick didn't do much fieldwork—he was mainly confined to his computer and the office—and he didn't know I required my operatives to check in frequently. It wasn't that I wanted to hamper their movements; it was a simple safety precaution to know where and with whom they were.

The Wiring Hall, I thought. Internet café on Chestnut Street. Maybe I'd catch up with him there.

I soon found I was playing follow the leader with Mick. The woman at The Wiring Hall told me she'd sent him to see a Mira Rasmussen at Zero's. Mira wasn't at Zero's, but after viewing my credentials the bartender gave me her address on nearby Francisco Street, a short distance from Fort Mason.

The building was three stories with an ornate arched

entryway and cracked marble floors, probably built in the thirties. Genteel shabbiness: the stucco façade needed painting, and the eaves and downspouts were rusted. The intercom was choked by static. Mira Rasmussen buzzed me in without using it.

*Trusting lady.*

Mira's apartment was on a second-floor corner. I had my ID out and ready when the slender, dark-haired woman opened the door. She wore an ankle-length floral-patterned skirt that flowed around her legs, and a pale pink tee; her eyes grew wide behind tortoiseshell-rimmed glasses as she examined my license.

"Another one," she said.

"I take it you've spoken with my associate, Mick Savage."

She nodded. "I'm glad you came by; I was just about to try to contact Mick because my friend Nola, who runs the bookstore down the block from Zero's, stopped in right after he left to give me the key to her flat so I can feed her cat while she's gone on vacation. I told her about meeting a real-life detective because she's a mystery novel junkie. Now I can tell her I've met two."

*Does this have a point?* I wondered. But you never want to crowd a witness.

"Anyway, Nola told me she saw the green-haired guy and a woman getting into a cab on the corner of Lyon and California, near Fort Mason."

"Did Nola describe the woman?"

"Yeah—sort of a retro hippie type. Dirty, dishwater-blond hair, long cape, sandals. I guess it was the same woman who was with him at The Wiring Hall. My friend said he didn't act as if he wanted to go with her; he looked kinda sick and she was holding him up and whispering in his ear."

"Could Nola hear anything?"

"Not much. Just something about a palace."

The Palace of Fine Arts, maybe. It was several blocks away from where the cab had picked Darcy and the woman up, on the edge of the Presidio.

I called the office, asked Derek to check with the cab companies about a pickup at Lyon and California. He called back within minutes: the fares—a man and a woman—had gone to the Palace of Fine Arts.

The neoclassical-style Palace, its dome rising against the clear blue sky, was mirrored in the lagoon that stretched beside it. The structure, which now housed the Exploratorium museum, had been built in 1915 for the Panama-Pacific International Exposition—a World's Fair that honored the opening of the Panama Canal and the four hundredth anniversary of the discovery of the Pacific Ocean. Where finely dressed ladies and gentlemen had once strolled under its huge rotunda, tourists now took pictures and children ran about, screeching and laughing at the echoes of their voices. Pigeons and gulls swooped through, wary eyes on the interlopers. Strangely for a city with such a homeless problem, there were only two shabbily dressed men curled on the marble floor with their bedrolls; a woman, face turned up to the sun, sat outside with her back against one of the Corinthian columns.

I began walking around, hoping to spot Darcy and the woman. Ducks floated on the placid water, diving under and wiggling their butts as they foraged for food. A man with a small boy diverted them with pieces of bread. The bell on an ice cream cart tinkled, and I bought a waffle cone with a scoop of vanilla chocolate chip from the red-haired vendor. I strolled along some more, watching the tour buses come and go, their occupants exclaim and click their cameras, and the sunbathers bask on the grass.

No Darcy. No woman.

When I returned to my starting point, the ragged homeless woman leaning against the column was still there. I approached her, thinking to ask if she'd seen anyone who resembled Darcy. Her skin was deeply wrinkled and browned, her beige parka stained and torn; she wore glasses with a cracked left lens; her eyes were open behind them.

"Ma'am?"

No answer.

I knelt down and gently touched a thin arm. The woman shifted the other way and fell over, her head thumping on the concrete.

*Jesus!*

Shaken, I momentarily drew back, then quickly felt for the woman's pulse.

Dead. Flesh still warm to the touch, but definitely dead.

Vomit had dribbled from the corners of her cracked lips, and her skin was bluish. Cardiac arrest. Or maybe a drug overdose. There were no outward signs of violence. She'd probably become disoriented, sat down here, and died.

Died alone and unnoticed in a public place, surrounded by the faded architectural beauty of another age.

I waited forty-five minutes at the Palace of Fine Arts for the uniforms and coroner's people to arrive. The city emergency services' response time was normally bad, and I supposed this call had been low-priority—after all, the woman was dead.

Briefly I'd considered telling the police that I thought my half brother might have been at the scene, then rejected the notion. There was no proof Darcy had come here and, as for my presence at the Palace, who could say that I wasn't there to enjoy a beautiful San Francisco afternoon?

I stood on the periphery of the official activities while the technicians did their work and plainclothes cops arrived. After a while a tall, sharp-faced man in a gray suit approached me, his light-brown hair ruffling in a sudden breeze: Inspector Chase Fielding of the SFPD Homicide detail. Homicide always came out in a case where death might not be natural. I'd never met the man, but I'd seen his picture in the *Chron* and Adah Joslyn, my operative who used to be on the elite squad, told me he was by-the-book but fair.

"Adah Joslyn speaks highly of you," Fielding said after he'd introduced himself.

"And of you."

"Tell her hello for me." He paused, surveying the scene at the Palace. "You found the body?"

"Yes. At first I thought she was just sleeping."

"Anyone else around?"

"A couple of homeless men with bedrolls inside the dome. They took off before I could ask them if they'd seen anything."

They'd been aroused by the commotion and vanished into the faceless population of those who wandered the city's streets and slept in its parks and other public places.

The police knew how homeless people sometimes established territories; they'd find them if it was at all possible.

Right now, my primary concern was Darcy.

Okay, they'd left, maybe gone to another palace.

They were grand residences, usually housing royalty or heads of state. Think Versailles, the Imperial Palace, Buckingham Palace, the Kremlin. Louis XIV, the emperors of Japan, the Tudors, the Romanovs. Nothing like that in this city.

What other palace was there? Of course—there was an art museum, the Palace of the Legion of Honor, in Lincoln Park across the Presidio and beyond the Sea Cliff district. Too far to walk, but Darcy and the woman could've caught the outbound 38 Geary bus that ran all the way to Point Lobos and the Veterans' Hospital. Or hailed another cab.

Who was this woman? As far as I was aware, Darcy knew no one in San Francisco; the closest he'd ever gotten was Berkeley.

But what did I really know of my half brother's life? He could've been to the city many times and not contacted me. Could've been living here since he left the Salmon River.

Inspector Fielding was through with me, so I headed for my car, a black BMW Z4 that used to belong to my best friend and sometimes operative, Rae Kelleher. Rae was also sort of family: she was married to my former brother-in-law—Mick's father—country music star and record producer Ricky Savage. Ricky had a horror of car accidents—both his parents and Rae's had died in them—and when he'd met Rae she'd been driving an ancient Nash Rambler, appropriately called the Ramblin' Wreck. He'd ridden in it only once before buying her a yellow Miata. A string of other cars, each one speedier but safer than the last, had followed yearly, and Rae had sold this latest to me last spring. My good luck: the Z4 had had fewer than five thousand miles on it when I took possession. I'd already added a couple of thousand.

Now I drove to Lincoln Park, at the northwest edge of the city. The Legion, a sprawling, colonnaded beaux arts building that took its name from the *Palais de la Legion d'Honneur* in Paris, loomed on its rise, beautiful but forbidding. Or perhaps that was only my overactive imagination kicking in: from the late 1860s to 1908 much of the surrounding land had been Golden Gate Cemetery, a potter's field. Although most of the bodies of the indigent or unidentifiable had then been relocated south to Colma, I remembered a grisly 1990s newspaper story about how coffins and skeletal remains that had been missed were unearthed during seismic retrofitting of the art museum.

It was nearing the museum's closing time. I parked and went up to the entrance. The lone ticket-seller—a woman whose pearls and cashmere sweater set suggested hers was a volunteer position—let me know immediately that I'd made the right decision in coming out here. She remembered Darcy well.

"He asked me where the cemetery was, and at first I didn't understand which one. But then I remembered the old potter's field that was relocated to Colma in . . . I don't know, a long time ago. But he said that wasn't the cemetery he was looking for. He started to become agitated—frankly, he didn't look as if he was feeling very well—and then the woman stepped in. A girl, really, from my perspective." Her eyes, in their webs of wrinkles, twinkled. "In her early to mid-twenties."

"Color of hair? Any distinguishing features?"

"Blond hair, not too clean. Her features were nothing outstanding. She was dressed as shabbily as he, but she was polite and very well-spoken. I gave her a list of other cemeteries—we keep them for people who are trying to decide where to inter their loved ones—and they left." She paused. "I felt sorry for them. He was crying, and the girl couldn't get him to stop. She said something to him...oh, what was it? These senior moments!"

"Take your time. I have middle-aged moments."

"Young woman, those are simply periods of distraction or forgetfulness. Keep your mind active, and you won't end up like me...oh, yes! Now I remember: the girl said, 'Laura told you that Gaby was dead and buried under a coral tree.' "

"Laura who, did she say?"

"No, just Laura."

"Are you sure the second name was Gaby? G-a-b-y?"

"Or b-b-y. Yes."

"Does the name hold any significance for you?"

"No."

"What's a coral tree?"

She smiled. "Interesting you should ask; we have one at our place on Maui. You usually find them in tropical or subtropical climates. Sometimes they're called flame trees, for their bright red flowers. They've been known to grow in this area, but they're very rare."

A coral tree in a cemetery. Laura. Gaby.

Not much to go on.

# Mick Savage

Colma, San Francisco's necropolis.

Sometimes called the City of Silence. Seventeen cemeteries, plus one for pets. The dead outnumbered the living by thousands. The number of memorial parks had burgeoned in the first decade of the 1900s, when San Francisco evicted all existing cemeteries from the city limits—greed for valuable real estate predictably trumping common decency.

Mick's lead to Colma had begun with a call from Shar: Darcy and the woman he'd been with on Chestnut Street had gone to the Legion of Honor, inquiring about cemeteries. Apparently someone named Laura had told Darcy that someone named Gaby was buried under a coral tree.

If that was a bona fide lead, he'd give up sex for Lent next year. As if that would ever happen...

A challenge, but he wasn't going to give up without an

all-out effort. He and Shar had long ago made a pact that when he performed the near-impossible, she treated him and a companion to dinner at a restaurant of his choice, provided it was within the city limits—damn, no Paris or Tuscany—and he'd had his sights set on The Sea Witch for months now.

Mick pulled his bike to the curb and went into a coffee shop. Ordered an espresso and asked the guy behind the counter what he knew about local cemeteries. The guy said he'd only lived there a week, had come up from LA to be near his sister. Mick went to a table, took out his BlackBerry. Searched for a cemetery with a coral tree. Nothing.

Okay, Gaby. Short for someone named Gabrielle who might be buried here? Try it. Several Gabrielles and Gabriellas buried at Cypress Lawn, Holy Cross, and the Italian Cemetery. Dates of death ranged from 1905 to 1999. One Gabriella at Crystal Springs Memorial Palace, died in October 2008—Gabriella DeLucci.

Palace. That fit. Now, if a coral tree was growing on its grounds...

Mick ran a quick check on Gabriella DeLucci. She'd died in 2008 at age eighteen. The cause of death was strangulation by person or persons unknown.

He went to the files of the SF *Chronicle*: on October 17, 2008, Gabriella DeLucci, heiress to an old San Francisco banking fortune, had been strangled, her body dumped near Elk Glen Lake in Golden Gate Park. There were a few more mentions of the murder over the next few months, and then nothing more. Next he checked Unsolvedmurders.com; the case had never been closed.

He'd check out the cemetery for her grave.

*     *     *

It was nearing five when he arrived at Crystal Springs Memorial Palace Cemetery. Perched on a knoll, it was incongruously close to a middle-class residential area that backed up on San Bruno Mountain State Park; the gates—rusted iron, hanging crookedly—were still open. He left his bike beside them and walked in on a rutted dirt track. There was a stucco building to the right, but it was shuttered and locked.

*Nobody around but us graves.*

He began wandering among them.

Old stones, going back to the mid-1800s. But no well-known local family names, such as Flood, Halladie, Crocker, or Sharon, were represented. Some graves with faded plastic flowers in urns; others with cracked head-stones and weeds growing up around them. A few old wooden grave markers, too weathered by the elements to read. Mick moved slowly, looking for Gabriella DeLucci's name.

Florence, beloved wife of...
Charles, our baby, aged two days...
Herman, devoted husband...
Matilda, angel mother...
Aurora, sleep in peace....

And then he saw the tree. Many spreading branches like an oak, and so short that some of them brushed the ground. A few brilliant red blossoms among its dark green leaves. He went over there and ducked into its shade.

Gabriella's marker was polished gray marble, a small slab flat on the pebble-covered ground. No urn, no flowers, nothing but the signs of infrequent maintenance. He knelt beside it, brushing away dried grass. Only her name and birth and death dates. No sentiment lost there.

After a moment he stood and looked around for the graves of other DeLucci family members, but he found none.

Now why was that? And come to think of it, why was Gabriella buried here? Seemed like an Italian Catholic family of prominence would have preferred Holy Cross or Cypress Lawn. Crystal Springs was small, a repository for the bones of the modest in financial and social standing— not a fitting resting place for members of families such as the DeLuccis.

Mick returned to Gabriella's grave. Squatted down and studied it. In a crease between the headstone and the dry earth lay a plastic object. A twisted red-white-and-blue drinking straw that looked as though it hadn't been there very long.

Odd thing to turn up in a cemetery, he thought.

And then he remembered what Mira Rasmussen had told him about Darcy's grabbing a handful of red-white-and-blue smoothie straws on his way out of The Wiring Hall.

Couldn't be. Or could it?

And if Darcy had been here and left the straw, why?

# Sharon McCone

In my office at the agency I rested my eyes from the computer monitor's glare. The pier loomed cavernously around me, silent, cold in spite of the baseboard heaters. Strange creaks and moans emanated from its far reaches. Out by the Golden Gate a foghorn bellowed. The fog would not come in tonight, I knew from long experience, but would hover offshore, close enough to set off the horns' deep-throated cacophony.

It was on a night like this that I'd been shot. I'd been on the catwalk outside my office, alone at night on a minor errand. Then I'd had the confrontation with the unseen intruder, the flash came from his gun—and I'd awakened to a different world, an altered life. Strange how less than three minutes could change your life forever.

Had something like that changed Darcy's life too? For Saskia's sake I hoped not.

I'd spent much of the early evening on my computer, trying to get a lead on him, but my skills weren't nearly as sharp as Derek's or Mick's, and all I'd accomplished was to frustrate myself and magnify my fears.

In many ways Darcy was such an innocent, and innocents wandering the streets of this city often came to bad ends. He had been at the Palace of Fine Arts at some point, but had he seen the dead woman? Fled? If so, to where? And what about the woman he'd been with?

And why, dammit, wasn't Mick keeping me informed?

I called his cell. No answer. Left an impatient message on voice mail.

On an impulse I called Inspector Chase Fielding. "The dead woman at the Palace of Fine Arts," I said without preamble, "have you identified her?"

If my call surprised him, his response didn't reveal it. "It was an easy ID: she was released from city jail yesterday, after doing two months for possession. Her name was Laura Mercer. No permanent address."

The ticket taker at the Legion of Honor had said something about the girl who'd been with Darcy talking about a Laura: "Laura told you Gaby is dead and buried under a coral tree."

Fielding said, "That name mean anything to you?"

Laura was a common name, popular for several generations; there didn't have to be a connection. And I didn't want to discuss my half brother's disappearance with the authorities—not yet.

"I know several Lauras—none of them with the surname Mercer. It was an overdose, right?"

"Appears to have been. We'll know more when we get the autopsy results."

Next month or two. The coroner's office was under-staffed and overworked.

"How old was she?" I asked.

"You saw her."

"It's hard to tell with druggies."

"The court records say thirty-two, although she looked fifty. May I ask what your interest in her is?"

"I found her body. Isn't that enough?"

"Well, you think of anything else, be sure to let me know."

The instant I ended the call with Fielding the phone rang again. Mick, finally.

"I've found out a bunch of stuff that we should go over tonight," he said, "but I'm on my way to Sea Cliff—Rae invited me to dinner and I promised her I'd come. And the battery on my laptop's losing its charge and I forgot my power cord, so I need to use her computer to verify some additional facts. Should I come by the pier or your house later?"

"Neither. I'll call Rae and ask her to set a third place at the table."

Rae's and Ricky's house was huge and, like most others in the exclusive neighborhood of Sea Cliff, it was built close to its neighbors, but tall hedges and lines of yew trees gave it privacy. Its three stories descended the bluff to a sand beach where it was nice to lie in the sun, although the water was too cold for swimming and the undertow wicked. There were six bedrooms on the house's top floor, an enormous living space on the second, and on the first a recording studio and what the adults privately referred to as the Hellhole—where Ricky's younger children stayed when they came up every other weekend from their mother's and stepfather's home in Bel Air to visit. Tonight the house's lights were muted.

Ricky was in New York for a few days, I knew, for talks with the head of a foundation he supported about organizing a nationwide concert tour to benefit breast cancer research. His older kids—Chris, Mick, and Jamie—were off pursuing their adult lives; the younger three—Brian, Lisa, and Molly—were at home with their mother and stepfather down south. And Rae was alone.

Well, except for the housekeeper and security staff. Mrs. Wellcome—a name both Rae and I found highly suitable and amusing—should by now be in her suite watching *Jeopardy!* Normally there was a security guard on duty: Ricky had a number of times been the subject of celebrity stalkings. As I got out of the car, a new guard whom I didn't recognize stepped from the shadows, identified himself, checked my ID, then allowed me to go inside.

Rae was in the living room, applying a match to the logs in the pit fireplace. When she sensed my presence she turned, smiling. She was short and slender with a mass of red curls falling to her shoulders, a sprinkling of freckles across her upturned nose—a feature that most people called "perky" and that she hated. Ricky had often told her that if she disliked it so much she should have cosmetic surgery—God knew they could afford it—but Rae had a horror of botched face-lifts, especially since one of her former teenage idols had emerged from one looking oddly lopsided.

"Mick's in my office, using the computer," she said.

"He tell you anything about what he's looking for?"

"No. Secretive as ever."

She provided wine, we settled in front of the fire, and I filled her in on the case.

"You're not sharing this information with the police, I take it," she said when I finished.

"Not yet."

"Did Saskia specifically ask you not to contact them?"

"No. But she has a long history of cleaning up Darcy's messes. He's really damaged, and she feels it's her fault."

"Maybe tough love is in order."

"Maybe. But that's not my decision to make."

"Are you sure he's so damaged, and not just intent on pissing everybody off? You know my history."

I did indeed.

Rae's drunken parents had died years ago in a fiery crash on the Pacific Coast Highway down in southern California. She'd only been eight years old, but they'd left her alone at their tiny house near Calabasas to take in a concert at the Topanga Corral. They must've hooked up with some other drunks and headed down to the coast; her father had lost control of their old VW bus and run head-on into a fuel tanker. Rae had been the only one home when the highway patrol officers arrived.

Her paternal grandmother in Santa Maria had grudgingly agreed to take her in—until a "suitable place" could be found for her. No such place materialized, and Rae lived in her grandmother's inhospitable household until her graduation from high school.

Did not live harmoniously, however. She'd been a devil as a child, out of control as a teenager. Anything she could do that would drive her grandma crazy was a worthy pursuit: her preferred manner of entering and exiting the house was by her bedroom window; sometimes she sneaked in boyfriends bearing beer; rock music and marijuana smoke filtered under her door; at meals she was sullen and silent.

Well, she sometimes claimed she'd been an ungrateful child, but from the first her grandmother had let her know she was an inconvenience she'd just as soon be rid of. "Your father's daughter but twice as bad" had been her favorite phrase.

There was the clatter of footsteps in the hallway, and Mick came into the room bearing a sheaf of papers. "Give me some of that," he said, gesturing at Rae's wineglass. "You have anything to nosh on?"

"No, but Mrs. Wellcome's chicken casserole is in the oven and the salad's crisping—"

"Fuck the casserole. And the salad. Going over this is more important."

Rae fetched him a glass of wine and a bag of salt-and-vinegar Kettle Chips.

"Okay," he said. Between sips and crunches, he proceeded to lay out the events of his day.

When he finished, I said, "This girl that Darcy was with at the Legion of Honor—we need to find out who she is. Also the one named Laura they'd apparently been talking to. Could be Laura Mercer, the woman I found dead at the Palace of Fine Arts today."

"I'll see what I can find out."

"What about the other woman they mentioned—Gaby?"

"That was tougher. You wouldn't believe how many Gabys, Gabrielles, and Gabriellas there are—and have been—in this world. But indexing them to a palace, a cemetery, and a coral tree narrowed the field, and I came up with one local possibility. I don't see what connection she might have had to Darcy, but there must be one because I found this on the grave."

He held up a red-white-and-blue straw, twisted into a little noose.

I closed my eyes, rejecting the evidence. But Darcy had that history of twisting small objects when under stress, and he'd snatched a handful of such straws from The Wiring Hall.

Mick went on, "At Crystal Springs Palace Cemetery there's a grave marker under a coral tree—one of the few such trees in northern California, according to my research—and the name on it is Gabriella DeLucci."

"And she was...?"

"An heiress who was murdered two years ago."

Gabriella DeLucci, Mick explained, had been the product of wealth and privilege: her great-grandfather Lorenzo DeLucci had emigrated from Sicily in 1841 and made his way west, arriving in time to stake a claim in the Sierra Nevada gold-mining country near Placerville. The vein that he tapped into was rich, and three years later he traveled to San Francisco, a town that had intrigued him upon his arrival in California, and used his gold-field proceeds to establish the Miners' Bank. DeLucci prospered, married into a well-to-do family, and settled into a Nob Hill mansion, high above the rough-and-tumble of old San Francisco's infamous Barbary Coast. He fathered one son, Lorenzo Junior.

Junior assumed control of the bank upon his father's death. The bank's assets continued to multiply, giving birth to branches throughout the city, and when Junior finally ceded his position to his son Laurence in 1975 it had branches in five Western states. Laurence married at thirty-two; Gabriella was his and his wife Marissa's only child. The couple died when a sightseeing hot air balloon in which they were riding caught fire and blew up over Salzburg, Austria. Gaby, as her friends called her, was twelve at the time.

"Leaving her as sole heir," I said. "Any other relatives who could've claimed a stake in the family fortune?"

"You mean relatives who might've wanted to kill her to get control? None."

"So what happened to her after her parents' death?"

"A director of the bank, Clarence Drew, was appointed her guardian. She went to boarding school—Miss Abbott's, an exclusive place on the Peninsula—and spent summers at Drew's lodge on Fallen Leaf Lake, up near Tahoe."

"And she died while she was at boarding school?"

"No. She'd graduated and was living in an apartment in Palo Alto and attending Stanford. On October seventeenth she was strangled and her body dumped up here in Golden Gate Park. The fact that she was at Stanford says she must've been pretty smart. And her obit says she was generous with both her fortune and time: praised her work on behalf of the homeless."

"What happened to the Miners' Bank? I don't remember seeing any of their branches in a long time."

"Bought out for mondo bucks by B of A after the DeLuccis died."

"Leaving Gaby a wealthy young woman. Who inherited from her?"

"A trust for homeless causes that she'd set up."

"And who administers the trust?"

"Clarence Drew."

"I'll talk with him tomorrow. Anything else I should know?"

"That's it for now."

"Okay. Good job so far."

"So far? Wow, thanks."

I yawned. Weariness had stolen over me, I realized all at once. I still tired easily. My recovery from locked-in syndrome was not yet complete. Where I'd been quick, I was sometimes sluggish. I became disoriented easily, forgetful. I'd grounded myself from flying because I couldn't maintain the concentration it requires. These were things that in time would right themselves, my neurologist assured me, but sometimes I wondered. Was this what it was like to age, grow feeble?

No, I kept telling myself, I was young, in the prime of my kick-ass life. But still I wondered.

Rae and Mick were giving me strange looks.

"Okay," I said briskly, "we'll continue this in the morning."

# Darcy Blackhawk

*I love you....* she'd said.

The little brown girl—that was how he thought of her, even if it was only the color of her cape—had tired of asking him questions he couldn't answer and a little while ago she'd slipped into bed with him. She was now curled up next to him, her breath warm on his cheek. Around them the house creaked and groaned. A narrow streak of light and faint talk and laughter and music filtered under the door.

The house—what did it look like? All he could picture was an old place and worn out. Tall, with lots of steps and a sharp, peaked roof.

Where was it? San Francisco someplace? Houses looked like that in the city.

He remembered coming here, tripping on the front steps, and her—what was her name?—holding him up. That was all.

But before...

Couldn't remember.

So much he couldn't remember, didn't understand.

He did remember the river, moving slow in the warm summer days. Rising moon, so bright, its light rippling toward the shore. High, higher than he'd ever been before. And then they'd come to him, whispering....

*Who?*

Them, just them.

The little brown girl sighed and touched his chin with her small hand.

All of a sudden he was afraid. Didn't want to be that close to anybody, much less this girl. Didn't want to be in this strange place either. Too confined, too airless, no stars or moon.

He moved away from her. Carefully slid out of the bed, so he wouldn't wake her. Funny—he had all his clothes on, and so did she, including the cape. The house had become quiet; maybe he could make his escape without running into anybody.

He tried to turn the doorknob. Locked. He bent and peered though the old-fashioned keyhole. Dark outside. He vaguely remembered the jingle of keys. Where could they be?

Not on the nightstand. The little brown girl must have them.

He went to the bed and looked down at her. She hadn't moved, didn't know he was leaving. Tentatively he touched her. Fast asleep. He ran his hands over the loose folds of the cape until they encountered a pocket, slowly fished the keys out. She still didn't stir.

*I love you....* she'd said. *I love you....*

# WEDNESDAY, SEPTEMBER 8

# Sharon McCone

Twenty past midnight by the time I got home.

I unlocked the door, disarmed the security system, felt the feline furballs twining around my legs before I could flick on the light.

Jessie and Alex, sister and brother. Shorthairs—Jessie black with white on her chest and paws, Alex completely black. Some miserable excuse for a human being had stuffed both of them into a Dumpster on a hot day last June, two little kittens that you could hold in the palm of your hand. They would have died if a passerby hadn't heard their frantic cries, rescued them, and delivered them to the SPCA shelter. Where Hy and I had fallen in love with the pair and brought them to—as the shelter employees called it—their "forever" home.

I went to the kitchen and checked their food bowls. Empty, but from the stray kibble on the floor I knew

that Michele Curley or her foster sister Gwen Verke had
come over from next door to feed them. Jessie and Alex
bumped against my legs again, mewling for something
else to eat.

"Con artists," I told them, then relented and put a little
more food in the bowls.

I'd had a message from Hy on my cell several hours
ago, but hadn't returned it because where he was it had
been the middle of the night. Now I calculated the time
for Switzerland—plus nine hours. Morning there, but
when I called, Hy's phone went to voice mail. In a meeting, I thought.

"Okay," I called to Jessie and Alex. "Time for bed."

A thump. Nothing more. But suddenly I was awake and
alert, attuned to danger. No matter that the security system was armed; even the best can be breached.

Another thump, on the deck above my ground-floor
bedroom.

I slipped out of bed and pulled on my robe, got Hy's .45
from his end table. My own weapons were, respectively,
in a lockbox upstairs and in the safe at the pier. I'm easily
separated from my firearms; Hy isn't.

I tiptoed up the spiral staircase.

Scrape...crash...clatter.

Whoever was out there was making one hell of a
racket. A person? Maybe a raccoon? They were all over
the city at night. Sometimes you saw them balancing
tightrope-walker style on the power lines.

A series of thuds and a grunt. Sounded like whoever
or whatever it was had fallen down the outside staircase.
I ran up the rest of the stairs, disarmed the alarm, then

eased out onto the deck. A tall figure was just turning onto the path between my house and the Curleys'. Footsteps slapped on the concrete, receded across the street.

Random prowler? Or someone who knew my address and wanted something from me? Well, it wasn't easy to keep addresses secret; a short time at the computer and even I could locate almost anyone, even download a photograph of the person's house. But I couldn't think of anything I had that anyone would want, and as far as I knew I was in no imminent danger from an enemy.

I retraced my steps onto the deck, reached inside to flip the switch for the floods. One of the canvas chairs lay on its side, and the seldom-used croquet set was tipped over, striped balls scattered on the planking. Charcoal had spilled from the bin next to the barbecue.

Clumsy, whoever it was.

I was about to go inside when I saw something lodged between the boards. Red, white, and blue. It was a plastic straw, bent and twisted into a knot.

Darcy.

He had a compulsive habit of calming himself by twisting things, and Mick had told me he'd found a straw like this on Gaby DeLucci's grave. So the prowler must have been Darcy. But why had he come skulking around in the dark? Why hadn't he just rung the bell?

I picked up the straw and stared at it as if it could tell me what he'd been doing here and why he'd run away after sending that e-mail message asking for help. The straw wasn't saying anything, so I went into the house and back to bed.

The cats had slept through the whole episode on Hy's pillow, but I was wakeful the rest of the night.

*        *        *

"I think your son is playing games with me," I concluded my narrative to Saskia. I'd called her as soon as I reached the pier a little before nine.

She sighed. "Well, at least he's still alive."

"He won't be if I find him."

"Sharon, he's—"

"I know—he's family."

"Well, he's not really your—"

"Sort of family, then, whether I like it or not. Don't worry. I won't kill him when I find him."

Families! Why did I have to have three, counting Elwood and the two malamute puppies he'd recently adopted?

I said to Mick, "You and Julia have now spent over four hours canvassing Tenderloin hotels and soup kitchens for Darcy. I've called around town to everybody who might have seen him. He hasn't contacted Robin or Saskia. There're no leads on the woman he was seen with. And, as far as I know, Laura Mercer has no connection to any of them."

"I think it's time we tried another tack."

"What?"

"The Gaby DeLucci case. The woman took Darcy to her grave. There must be some connection."

"Sounds to me like that's going off on a tangent."

"What else have we got?"

"... You're right."

At two o'clock that afternoon I was in the waiting room of the offices of Clarence Drew, Gaby DeLucci's former guardian.

The DeLucci Foundation had a suite on the forty-ninth floor of 555 California Street, formerly the Bank of America Tower. I had hurried up the wide steps to the plaza, past the black granite sculpture titled Transendence but locally nicknamed The Banker's Heart. To me it has always resembled a turtle shell, reptiles being as cold-blooded as financiers.

The foundation's suite was not a large one, but it was well appointed: thick beige carpets, leather furnishings, good lamps, and an elaborate tansu chest, which I envied, having recently developed an interest in Japanese furnishings.

Clarence Drew had said he could spare me fifteen minutes before his luncheon appointment. I was on time, but he kept me waiting twenty-five. When his assistant ushered me into his office I momentarily focused on the sweeping Bay view, then gave my attention to the man seated behind the desk.

*My God, he looks like Edward G. Robinson!*

The slightly protuberant eyes, heavy jowls, wide nose, and thick lips were an uncanny match for the actor's features. His voice, however, was all his own. It squeaked.

"Be seated, Ms. McCone." He motioned to a leather chair across from him.

Not courteous enough to rise or shake hands. A man in an expensive office and well-tailored suit, who didn't fit either of them well.

"You have fifteen minutes," he added, tapping his cuff, under which his watch presumably resided.

I sat. The chair was harder than it looked and the impact jarred my spine.

"As I told your appointments secretary," I said, "I'm a

private investigator hired to look into the circumstances of the death of your former ward, Gabriella DeLucci."

"Hired by whom?"

"I'm sorry, that's confidential."

Drew leaned back in his chair and folded his hands on his considerable belly. "Many people have been interested in Gabriella's death, mainly for sensational reasons."

"My client has no intention of exploiting her story."

He raised his thick eyebrows, waiting.

Different tack. "I assume you'd like to see Gabriella's killer brought to justice."

"Of course."

"Then perhaps you could share with me what you remember about her murder."

The last word made Drew flinch. His gaze turned inward for a few moments. Then he blinked, focused on me again, and said, "Perhaps you should share your client's motivations with me."

"There's been a new development in the case, something connected with a missing relative of my client. That's as much as I can tell you."

He leaned forward in his chair. "What sort of new development?"

"I'm sorry. Privileged information."

"Privileged." Drew slumped back into his chair, the word ending in a sigh that made his big lips quiver. "A word that also applies to Gaby."

"How so?"

"She wanted for nothing her whole life. She was sheltered and catered to by her parents, and I admit I did no more to instill knowledge of the real world in her than they did. I loved the girl, but sometimes her naïveté exasperated me, and I had to remind myself that I was partially responsible for it."

"In what way was she naïve?"

He spread his hands. "In every way. She had no concept of the value of money; she thought it simply poured from a fountain into her hands. She trusted everyone, even the most dubious of individuals. It's no wonder she got herself killed."

*Got* herself killed?

*Blame the victim.*

I must have looked disturbed, because Drew said, "No, I didn't mean that the way it sounded, but it's so difficult to watch someone you care for set out on a path toward her own destruction."

"Tell me about these 'dubious' characters she trusted."

"They were mostly homeless people. People who checked in and out of a shelter she volunteered for while she was in high school."

"Which shelter was that?"

"St. Francis Relief, on Folsom near Seventh."

"Do you recall any of the homeless people she associated with, perhaps trusted more than others?"

"Only a few names she mentioned in postcards to us while we were at the lake, and they were obviously assumed. Lady Laura, Tick Tack Jack, and the . . . somebody . . . oh, yes—the Nobody."

Lady Laura. Laura Mercer?

"This Laura—what did Gaby say about her?"

"Only that she was a prostitute who was 'getting her act together.' "

"Did she tell you her last name?"

"No."

"Or what she looked like?"

"No. I never so much as saw any of those people."

"And the others? What did she say about them?"

"...She was helping the Jack person wean himself off methamphetamines. The Nobody had unspecified mental problems."

"Did she mention anything more specific about any of them?"

"No. She wasn't very forthcoming. But she gave up on that work before she moved to the apartment in Palo Alto and started at Stanford."

"Was she renting the apartment alone or with a roommate?"

"With a friend from Miss Abbott's. Lucy Grant. They'd known each other since kindergarten. She's Lucy Bellassis now. I know because I noticed her wedding announcement in the newspaper."

"Bellassis? Any relation to the aircraft leasing people?"

"Yes. Lucy's husband, Parker, is CEO of the company. I gather he inherited it from his father."

"Do you know how I can locate her?"

"I lost track of the people from Gaby's life years ago."

"How long did Gaby live in Palo Alto?"

"Only two months or so, and then I had a call...."

Drew bowed his head, arms outstretched on the desk. After a moment he looked up. "I had a call," he repeated, "and my world changed forever."

I knew about that kind of call: one had come when my brother Joey died of an overdose in a shack near an old lumber-company town in Humboldt County; another when Pa died, happily involved in the woodworking he had so loved.

I said, "I've asked the SFPD for the case file on Gaby's murder, but perhaps you could tell me about it from your personal perspective?"

Drew folded his hands on his paunch. "Well, as I said, there was the call. My wife, Marian, was at our Tahoe place for the week, so I rushed alone to Golden Gate Park...Elk Glen Lake. By that time they'd removed her body from the water—she was caught in the reeds at the narrower end of the lake—and put her on a gurney. She... hadn't been dead long but I had a difficult time making a positive identification. Gaby alive was so animated, Gaby dead was...nothing. The rest of it—the police interviews, their search of her room at our house and her apartment in Palo Alto—are just a blur. Because of her disfiguring injuries, there was no viewing, just a small graveside service."

"Did the police question any suspects?"

"Very few. Homeless people who were known to frequent the Elk Glen Lake section of the park. But Gaby wouldn't have gone there alone at night."

"So she was killed in Palo Alto or somewhere else in the city, and her body abandoned in the lake. By someone she knew, possibly."

"Or a stranger. The police talked with her friends, of course, but none of them could actually be termed suspects."

"What about Gabriella's movements before her death? Where had she been, who had she seen, what had she been doing?"

"Gaby attended her ten o'clock seminar at Stanford and later had lunch with an old classmate from Miss Abbott's here in the city, but after that no one could place her."

"Did she have a car?"

"Of course—one of those small Mercedes convertibles. It was in its space at the apartment building until I finally had it towed away and sold. I took care of all the arrangements, and I'm still administering her trust according to her wishes."

Drew sighed heavily. "After that...we went on. The updates from the police became less frequent and now have stopped. We were left with a big hole in our lives. My wife never got over it; sometimes I'd come home and find her sitting in the dark in Gaby's old room."

Drew's mouth twitched and he swallowed as if to remove a bad taste. "Gaby ruined our lives. I know that sounds harsh, but in some way she brought her murder upon herself. I loved her, but I hate her for what she did to us."

*Yes, blame the victim.*

# Darcy Blackhawk

*Nobody can find out what I did.*

He lay shivering under a big bush. Its leaves dripped water on him. There was a steady thrum of traffic close by. It hardly ever stopped, hurt his head. He pressed his hands to his ears but the noise came through anyway.

How'd he gotten here? When?

That little brown girl...taking her keys while she slept, turning the lock and sneaking out of the bedroom. It was a downstairs room behind a garage; stairs led up from there. He tiptoed up them and pushed the door at the top open a few inches. Dark, quiet house. The hallway led to a front door.

He crept to it, turned the knob. Locked, but one of the other keys on the ring might open it. He tried them—one, two, three—

And then he was out on the porch in the cold night air. Running down the steps and away from there, squinting in the bright lights, stumbling on the uneven sidewalk, darting across the streets. Cars honking at him...and then the dark ahead...

Now light was coming through the branches over his head. Not bright, but enough to make his eyes sting. He'd cover them, but if he did he'd have to take his hands off his ears, and then that damned traffic roar...

Sick now. Retching. Vomit spilling out of his mouth and across his cheek onto the ground.

*Sit up! You'll choke!*

Sitting. Better.

He'd done something, couldn't remember what, but he had a feeling it was bad.

*Think!*

He flashed on the cold, dead face.

*No, don't wanna go there.*

But it was bad, very bad. Or was it? *Had* he done something?

Where had he been since then?

Shar's house.

Was going to knock on the back door, but he'd tripped and fallen down. Something crashing, those balls rolling everyplace. Lights on in the house next door. He'd had to run before somebody saw him and called the cops.

But where'd he run to?

He pushed to his feet, water from the leaves running down his cheeks. Felt sick again, bent over till it passed. Then he stumbled through the bushes, a branch scratching a corner of his eye, and came out on a street. Something about the light told him it was afternoon.

Bicycle shop, small café, instant printers, real estate office. He didn't remember seeing any of them before.

He started across the street, and a car rushed past, almost grazing him.

*Got to get hold of Shar. Need her.*

But now he couldn't remember where she lived. Couldn't remember her phone number either.

Her e-mail address? He remembered that...didn't he?

*sharon@mcconeinvestigations.com.*

Yeah, right, that was it. Okay, find a place with free computer terminals, like before.

He moved along the sidewalk, gazing into windows, until he found one. Went and typed, "Real trouble now. Help me."

She'd get back to him now. He was sure she would.

When he went outside—the waitress glaring at him for not buying anything—a picture in the real estate agency's window caught his eye. Old house, tall, with marble steps.

*The little brown girl.*

*What I did.*

*Nobody can find out what I did.*

# Sharon McCone

Real trouble now. Help me."

The message jarred me. For a moment I sat very still, absorbing it. Then I fired it off to Derek, with a request he find its source. A few minutes later he got back to me: Beans, a Haight Street café.

The Haight had changed since hippie days, yet not changed. It was a neighborhood trying to immortalize its brief glory, when it had been featured in national magazines as home to the counterculture. Head shops still remained, wannabe hippies still loitered on its sidewalks, but the scene was shopworn, much like the souvenir stands at Fisherman's Wharf. And in between were interesting boutiques and good restaurants; on the hill above were multimillion-dollar homes. Another neighborhood that would reinvent itself again and again—as most of those in this city did.

The woman on the counter at Beans remembered Darcy—he was a "cheapskate," she said. "And weird."

I had to agree.

"Did you see where he went after he left here?"

"No."

"D'you remember anything else about him?"

"He looked scared. A druggie needing a fix or afraid his connection was gonna hit him for money he owed."

Was that it? Or was it something more complex?

Either way, Darcy seemed farther away than ever.

I walked slowly along Haight Street, hoping to spot Darcy. A man in a dashiki with paint on his face was playing a drum. He ignored me when I tried to talk with him. A circle of teenagers sat on the sidewalk near Magnolia's—great burgers—sharing a joint. They looked at me as if *I* were the freak when I approached them. No, they hadn't seen anybody like my half brother.

Would they even notice? I wondered.

A clown was selling balloons on the corner of Haight and Stanyan, across from Golden Gate Park. Momentarily I shied away from him: I have an unreasonable dislike of both clowns and mimes—unfortunate because they abound in San Francisco. Then I steeled myself and asked about Darcy. The clown said he hadn't seen him.

My fear for Darcy was coming upon me in waves now—ebbing when I approached a new prospect, flowing when each answered in the negative. Repeatedly I checked my phone and e-mail. Nothing of any consequence.

*Real trouble now.*

A person with Darcy's history would know real trouble when he encountered it. He'd been to Beans, sent me a message, and...?

Disappeared again. Or been forced to disappear. Either way, he was gone.

# Mick Savage

Earlier this afternoon Shar had turned over to him the information from her interview with Clarence Drew, then left to pursue a lead on Darcy. He was reluctant to start work on the cold case that might or might not be connected to Darcy's disappearance. Maybe, wherever she'd gone, she'd find her half brother and that would be that.

In the meantime she'd saddled him with the dubious task of trying to find three homeless people with the equally dubious names of Tick Tack Jack, Lady Laura, and the Nobody. St. Francis Relief, on Folsom near Seventh Street, would be his starting place.

It was an old hotel, three stories of ugly stucco, its windows barred and in some instances boarded up. Mick went inside, to a foyer with walls papered in posters advertising free clinics, odd jobs, medical marijuana clubs, shelters, church counseling groups, and any number of other services. Many were fringed at the bottom with tags with phone numbers written on them, but there had been few takers. To his right was the old registration desk, strewn with more flyers, and to his left a common room filled with shabby mismatched furnishings. A woman— dark-haired, anorexically thin—sat at a card table, pecking at the keys of an old Selectric typewriter.

"Hello," Mick said from the doorway.

She didn't look up, although a slight change in her posture indicated she'd heard him.

He went into the room. "Excuse me."

"I know you're there." She remained focused on the keyboard.

"That's right, I'm here."

"Damn!" A sigh. Big brown eyes looked up at him. "This is a referral form for one of our clients to a state agency. It needs to be perfect, but I've screwed up three copies now."

"I'm sorry for interrupting you."

"Not your fault. I'm a lousy typist." She released the sheet from the typewriter, balled it up, and flung it at a wastebasket. It missed.

"I happen to be a very good typist," Mick said. "I do better on a computer, but I used to have one of those machines. I'm sure I could familiarize myself fast enough."

"But this is confidential—"

"I know all about confidentiality." He crossed the room, handed her his card. Her collarbone was prominent, and through her thin red sweater he could see the outlines of her ribs.

She was looking closely at the card. Then she looked closely at him. "You want something?"

"Just information on three former clients."

"I can't give you that."

"It's old information. The clients may benefit if I can locate them. A mentor has asked us to locate them."

The big eyes grew wider. "This mentor wants to help them?"

"Right."

"Oh, that's wonderful! Give me the names and I'll look for their files."

"And in the meantime, I'll type your form."

As he sat down at the card table and tried to remember how the damned Selectric worked, he felt bad about lying to her.

# Sharon McCone

Paper reports," Mick said, dropping an armload of folders on my desk. "St. Francis Relief is so underfunded they don't have a computer. They do have a copy machine, an old one, and I've been sweating over it for hours."

Mick had told me about the homeless organization and warned me he'd be bringing the documents. It was well after three o'clock, and my eyes burned from staring at my monitor as I'd read other operatives' reports and intermittently tried to get a lead on Darcy's whereabouts. I eyed the files with distaste.

"Have you read these?" I asked.

"No, but the lady who provided them gave me an overview."

He had that expectant look—the one that said I should commend him for his diligence and his ability to get the best out of ladies who were attracted to him. But I wasn't in the mood to banter with him. It had been a frustrating day, and my sense of humor had taken a battering.

"Sit down and tell me what you've got."

He flopped into one of the chairs. "Leads on all three of the people Gaby DeLucci was mentoring. Tick Tack Jack—real name Jack Tullock—kicked his meth habit and moved to Oregon. Runs a ranch he calls The Jokin' Jack near a little town, Amity, in Yamhill County. Raises wine grapes."

"How could a meth addict on relief afford that?"

"An uncle left the ranch to him after he moved to Oregon and got clean and sober. Details are in the file."

"Lady Laura?"

"You were right—her full name was Laura Mercer. Her background's more sketchy than Tullock's. Was born in Chicago, parents deceased. No evidence of a high school diploma or higher education. There's a record of her being employed as a domestic in the Boise area until four years ago. As you know, her most recent residence was the city jail."

Boise. Maybe she had known Darcy there?

"And the Nobody?"

"He's the most interesting of the three."

The Nobody, Mick explained, was a former blues guitar player named Chuck Bosworth. He'd been moderately popular throughout the Bay Area until two years ago, when he'd suffered a minor stroke that affected the motor functions in his hands. Now he occasionally turned up on open mike nights at seedy clubs, billing himself as the Nobody and banging on his old guitar while singing off-key.

"Nobody sightings" had become popular with a cult of old blues fans, and they'd established a website to chronicle them. Bosworth moved around among SRO hotels in San Francisco and Oakland, and Mick had found no current address for him.

"Okay," I said. "Jack Tullock may remember something about Gaby and the others. You contact him. I'll tackle Chuck Bosworth. And you ask Derek to keep on trying to find out who the woman Darcy was at the cemetery with was."

"She's proving impossible to trace."

"Then we'll work these other angles, tangential as they might seem."

I pulled the Chuck Bosworth file from the bottom of the stack, but before I opened it I went to NobodySightings .com.

Bosworth was a heavyset black man who, at the time the photo that was featured on the site had been taken, was in his fifties. Over the course of his career he'd made three CDs that were offered through the site for two dollars apiece plus postage from a recording company called BluesSynch. There were various comments from fans: "Awesome, man." "One of the greats." "Should've had a terrific career."

I clicked on the list of recent sightings. The Aces Club on Mission Street; Our Hideaway near Oakland's Jack London Square; CopOut in Daly City; the corner of Seventh and Market; Hair o' the Dog on Silver Avenue; Van Ness near Turk Street; Lydia's Lounge in southern Sonoma County; M&M's Lounge in the Mission.

The Nobody got around.

I needed an expert, so I called The Library Hotel in New York City, where Ricky was staying that week, and caught him just before he was to leave for the airport.

"Chuck Bosworth?" he said. "Good blues musician. Not one of the best, but he had his day. I heard someplace that he's gone off the rails and is singing for nickels and dimes."

"Right. You have any idea who he hangs out with, where he might be living?"

"No, but I can make some calls."

The music world, like that of any other profession, has its own intricate connections: any given person, no matter his status or whereabouts, is only a few calls away. I was reminded of the Moccasin Telegraph, a sort of World Wide Web of Indians who communicate information via any means available to them.

I thanked Ricky and hung up, then swiveled back to the computer screen and clicked through my address book to the listing for my friend Will Camphouse, the creative director of an ad agency in Tucson. Will and I might or might not be related, bloodlines among the tribes being tangled as they are, but we'd formed a bond similar to that of brother and sister when I was searching for my birth parents.

"Hey, you," he said in his easy Southwestern manner. "How's it goin'?"

"Not too well. You remember my half brother, Darcy?"

"Couldn't forget him."

I explained what had been going on, ending with, "It occurred to me that this might be something to put out on the Telegraph."

"I'll be glad to do it. When're you gonna learn how?"

"I already have. I call you, and you call Aunt Bessie, who lives in Salmon, and she calls her friend Dorothy, who works for the Department of Forestry, and she calls—"

"Smartass."

"I love you too."

I sat in my ratty old armchair by the arched window and stared out at the Bay, mentally running through the bits and pieces of information that we'd gathered so far. They were puzzling, inconsistent, yet I sensed connections beneath their surface.

Number one: Lady Laura's death. Was it connected to Gaby DeLucci's murder, or was it merely coincidental? Was it somehow connected to Darcy?

Number two: this blaming of the victim. Yes, when people died those left behind were frequently angry with them. Natural response, one of the stages of grief. But Clarence Drew had been so vehement, so insistent that Gaby had brought her murder upon herself.

Number three: Drew's recall of Tick Tack Jack, Lady Laura, and the Nobody had been too quick, considering they were just people Gaby had mentioned in postcards. Had they featured prominently in the police investigation? I'd have to check when the file I'd requested from the SFPD arrived.

Number four: Lucy Bellassis. She was a living link to Gaby.

After a while I turned to the computer and accessed the Bellassises' address and phone number. Turned out they were in Sea Cliff, a couple of blocks from Rae and Ricky. Easy enough to pay a call later on.

# Darcy Blackhawk

*Out here nobody looks at me.*

He stumbled on the broken sidewalk, and still nobody noticed him.

There was a pizza place, burger and sandwich shops. He smelled Indian food. His stomach rumbled, but he had no money.

Head shop, patchouli oil overpowering the cooking smells. Books, ice cream. Crafts and beads. Someplace called Magnolia's. A lot of regular people, a lot of freaks like him. None of them paid attention to anybody else.

In front of a newsstand a bunch of kids sat on the sidewalk. One of them had brighter green hair than his. They wore ripped jeans and ratty T-shirts and none of them could've been over eighteen. Suburban kids, he could tell. They had warm dinners and cozy beds to go home to when they wanted. He'd had that once too. No more.

His own fault. But he couldn't go back to Mom's, not after what he'd done.

Darcy went over and sat down on the sidewalk. One of the kids said, "Hey."

"Hey." He leaned back against the building's wall. It was still warm from the sun, although dark was setting in above the hills.

The kid scooted closer. "Somebody's been lookin' for you."

"Who?"

"Pretty lady. Dark hair. Old, though. Got to be in her thirties."

Shar. She was in her early forties, but looked younger. So she'd gotten his message. But why hadn't she—oh, yeah, he didn't have his laptop any more and the e-mail in his head wasn't working.

The kid said, "If the sit/lie goes through, we're all in trouble."

"The what?"

"Fuckin' city's trying to pass a law that we can't sit or lie on the sidewalks. That happens, they'll bust all of us. My dad, he says I get busted, he's not gettin' me out. Says I can rot in jail. You been in jail, man?"

"Yeah."

"Where?"

He didn't remember. "Lots of places."

The kid looked impressed. Darcy closed his eyes, turned his face up to the sun.

"Wow. I hear the guards beat you up. The other prisoners bugger you."

He sort of nodded off. When he opened his eyes the

kid was still staring at him. Darcy said, "Don't go to jail if you can help it."

"I can take it."

"Sure you can, kid."

"Well, I can! You got any dope on you?"

"No."

"Know where me and my buddies can score?"

"No."

"How come? You look like you're on something."

He had been, but he'd come down. Way down.

He said, "Go away. Just go away and leave me alone."

It was full dark, and the kids had disappeared. He was starving. His leg was cramped from sitting on the cold sidewalk, and he got up and limped along the street. At one corner he found a dime, and at mid-block a quarter. He kept going, snout to the ground like a fucking snuffling pig.

Animal, that's what he was. Smelly, vicious animal.

With the quarter he could call Mom collect. But why would she accept the charges? He could call Shar....

No, he couldn't. She'd turn him in to the cops when he told her what he'd done. He couldn't take jail, not again. He'd better keep walking.

*Out here nobody looks at me.*

# Sharon McCone

The most recent Nobody sighting had been at a bar called M&M's Lounge on Valencia Street in the Mission district. I knew M&M's from when I'd lived a few blocks away on Guerrero Street: it had been there forever, a grimy hold-out against the high-end clubs that had sprung up in the area. Developers had tried to unseat the owners, Mario and Madeline Traverso, but with no luck. The couple had been operating their establishment since the early seventies, and would continue to do so until either they or their last regular customer died.

Cocktail time. I headed for my old neighborhood.

The Mission district used to be an Irish and Italian working-class neighborhood. Then came the Latinos, who enlivened the scene there with their bodegas, salsa music, and colorful murals. Later, addicts and drug dealers infested the area. The most recent incursion was of hip, affluent people—some called them the bridge-and-tunnel crowd, since they mainly hailed from the suburbs—drawn to the Mission by a profusion of relatively inexpensive restaurants and nightclubs.

No suburbanite would ever set foot in M&M's.

Outside it was grimy, with a glass-block window shielding its interior from passersby. Inside it was dark, and you had to pass through a red velvet curtain that smelled of dust and mildew. Black leatherette booths, a few tables, and a long bar covered with water stains from the drinks of generations. Mario—tall, thin, and bald with thick glasses and a hearing aid—presided in the lull before the evening rush. Two old men sat at the far end of the bar, rolling dice for drinks. I slipped onto a stool. Mario looked away from the TV mounted on the far wall, recognized me, and smiled.

"Sharon McCone. Maddy and me'd about given up on you. Don't come around to your old haunts much any more."

M&M's had never been a "haunt" of mine, but when I'd been with All Souls Legal Cooperative I'd worked out a couple of minor problems—deadbeat checks—for Mario and his wife.

I said, "Don't get around much, period."

"Nonsense. I hear about you all the time." He leaned toward me, lines beside his eyes crinkling with concern. "You got married. Not to that asshole, I hope."

"Which one?" My taste in men before Hy had been iffy, to say the least.

"Well, the cop was okay, but the diddlyboppin' one with the gold Jag was kinda flaky."

*Diddlyboppin'?* Oh, right—Don DelBoccio, the disk jockey.

"What happened to him?" Mario asked.

"He got a better job in Denver."

"And the cop?"

"Got married and retired to the Gold Country."

"So who's this one? I see he didn't give you a wedding ring."

"I'm not wearing it tonight. On the job, you know."

Mario nodded and winked conspiratorially. "This one a good guy?"

"The best."

"I heard about you getting shot in the head. Hell of a thing. You okay now?"

"I'm good, thanks."

"Relieved to know it. What'll it be?"

"Draft beer, whatever you recommend."

Damn, he brought me a Bud.

"Mario," I said, "you remember a character named Chuck Bosworth? Blues guitarist, lately calls himself the Nobody."

"Yeah I do. Had to throw him outta here the other week—was bothering my customers with his cater-wauling."

"He's really that bad?"

"That bad and then some."

"But once he was good."

"He had a so-so talent."

"D'you know where he's living now?"

Mario shook his head. "I don't, but one of my regulars might. Guy calls himself Jimmy Crow."

"Jimmy Crow?"

"Not his real name. These old guys, they like to go by what they call 'handles.' None of them's who he says he is, none of them's got a past. 'Course, most of 'em got a good reason to lose their history."

"What's Jimmy Crow's?"

"Who knows? Whyn't you ask him? He comes in right about eight every night, depending how good his watch is working."

I didn't want to sit in the bar and wait till eight for Crow's appearance, so I went out to my car and made a call to Lucy Bellasis. She sounded mildly tipsy on the phone, but when I told her I was interested in the Gaby DeLucci case she urged me to come to her house.

The Bellassis home was a huge white pile of stucco and cornices and balconies and columns atop a rise covered in immaculately trimmed, unbelievably green grass. I'd driven past it many times on my way to Rae's and Ricky's house and had always wondered how anyone could live comfortably in such a grandiose structure.

Lucy was tall and overly slender, with dark hair and gray eyes and delicate features. She looked far too young and casual to be mistress of such a large, formal home. Her jeans were ripped—although they had probably cost a small fortune—her green sweater was tight enough to show the outlines of her ribs, and her pointy-toed cowboy boots looked new and shiny. She held a goblet of white wine in one hand—a *big* goblet.

"Come in, come in," she said. "I'm so glad for the company. Park—that's Parker, my husband—is away, and this mouse wants to play." She hiccupped, said, "Oops, sorry!" and giggled.

*Oops is right. What have I gotten myself into?*

The house's marble-floored entry was enormous, with a large round table topped by a vase of red roses in its center and fragile-looking chairs that probably nobody ever sat in along the sidewalls. Archways opened into a labyrinth of other rooms, and a wide staircase curved up the rear wall to the second story. Lucy led me into a vast, brightly lighted living room where every lamp was ablaze, and briefly I wondered if the woman was afraid to be home alone. Of course, she wasn't totally alone; a place like this would require a platoon of live-in help. No, I decided, the lights were all on simply because the Bellassises could afford enormous utility bills.

The living room was not as formal as the entry: one wall was covered with a large entertainment center, the other with a wet bar; the furnishings were of soft, buttery leather. Lucy went to the bar and poured me a glass of wine without asking if I wanted any, then topped off her own.

"Park's gone a lot," she said, flopping into the chair next to the one she'd indicated I should take, "and I get lonely."

"I imagine his business requires a lot of travel," I said.

"No, he just wants to get away from me." Before I could process the remark, much less reply, she switched the subject. "You said on the phone that you'd like to talk about my friend Gaby."

"Yes—"

"Don't tell me Clarence is actually paying to find out who killed her."

"No—"

"'Cause when she died he sure wanted to make the

whole thing go away in a hurry. Gave me orders to pack up all the stuff she had at our apartment and either give it to charity or throw it out. Demanded her tuition back from Stanford. Had her car towed away. And that place where he had her buried, have you seen it?"

"No, but—"

"Awful, dinky little cemetery, nobody who's anybody is buried there." Her features grew mournful. "Not too many people came to the service, either because Clarence didn't invite them or they couldn't find the place."

"What d'you think of Clarence Drew?"

She glowered, hatred overcoming grief. "He's an ugly, two-faced little man who never gave a shit about Gaby. He tried to stay on her good side, because he wanted her to keep him on as executor of her parents' trust so he could collect his fat salary. But she told me a couple of weeks before she died that she was thinking of making some changes and had made an appointment with a lawyer."

"What kind of changes?"

"That she didn't say. Gaby was a private person when it came to money."

"Who was the lawyer?"

"Somebody big. Usually does criminal cases, but he took Gaby on because he was a friend of her father's from way back. Give me a minute." She put her fingers to her brow. "Bible name . . . That's it—Solomon. You know, Solomon and Sheba."

I had an attorney friend named Glenn Solomon, but he didn't practice family law. "You don't know his first name?"

She shook her head. "Gaby said he'd roomed with her father in college."

"What was your relationship with Gaby like?"

"God," Lucy said, "just thinking about it makes me miss her. We were so close—like sisters, since childhood—and we had such great times. Traveled, went on ski trips, decorated our apartment. We smoked our first joint together, got our first periods the same week. Driver's licenses too. When she died my life seemed so empty."

"Did you have other mutual friends? A group you went around with?"

"Not really. You know how tight some people can be? Like they understand each other, and there's no room in the world for somebody else?"

I didn't; even though Hy and I were close—at some times seemed to have a telepathic connection—there had always been space in my life for others.

I said, "Tell me about Gaby."

The front door opened. There were footsteps and a woman looked into the room. She was short, dressed in a blue sweatshirt and a long, chaotically patterned skirt whose colors didn't match the shirt's, and her scuffed sandals revealed dirty-looking feet. Her hair was pushed up and covered by a red tam. A man joined her: tall, heavily built, in jeans and a leather jacket that had seen better days. His longish blond hair hung down over his forehead.

"Lucy?" the woman said. "Everything okay?"

"Of course. Why?"

"Well, you look kind of stressed."

"I'm fine. What're you doing here?" Lucy hadn't appeared stressed to me, even though she'd been talking about Gaby. Now frown lines appeared and the area around her lips whitened.

"Need to use Park's computer," the woman said. "Who's your guest?"

Lucy introduced me. The young woman was Torrey Grant, Lucy's older sister. The man was Jeff Morgan, one of Bellassis Aviation's charter pilots.

Lucy said to Torrey, "Did Park say it was all right to use his computer?"

"I always do."

"That's not what I'm asking."

Torrey's stance became defensive. "Well, I *do*."

Lucy sighed. "Go ahead then."

The two turned and went upstairs.

Lucy muttered, "She's such a pain in the ass."

"In what way?" I asked.

"All ways. But that's another story. Let's just say she's like an invasive plant, sending up shoots everywhere."

"Some people," I said, thinking of Darcy, "are expert at worming their way into others' lives. Once they're in, they wiggle around till they take up too much room. Then they're hard to dislodge."

"That's Torrey." Obviously upset, she excused herself and poured some more wine, held the bottle up questioningly to me. I shook my head.

"So," Lucy said, sitting down again, "back to Gaby."

"Yes, tell me more about her."

"She was funny and adventurous. She took flying lessons with me, then got into skydiving. Park was running his father's FBO at Oakland Airport, that's where we met him."

FBO: fixed base of operation. They offer aircraft tie-downs and rentals, fueling, flight training, charters, aircraft sales. Other services range from the basic—restrooms and telephones—to the luxurious—pilots' lounges, exceptional customer service, conference and flight-planning centers, crew sleeping quarters. The Bellassis operation had recently moved from Oakland to SFO, where its facility was reputed to rival that of Signature, the top FBO worldwide.

Lucy went on, "Gaby, she was generous; if you admired something of hers, all of a sudden it was yours. She was beautiful but, you know, she didn't let it get in the way. Park fell in love with her at first sight. It wasn't until she died that he even looked at me." Her face grew melancholy, and she looked down at her left hand, where diamond wedding and engagement rings caught the light.

"It wasn't a love match between Park and me. We were both grieving so badly for Gaby. I guess that's our strongest bond. And going on as we were—staying in college, planning careers—seemed so pointless. I mean, if it happened to her, who was to say it wouldn't happen to us?"

My skin prickled. Something there.

"Why would you think the same thing might happen to you?"

"...Well, life's fragile, isn't it? There's really nothing and no one you can wholly trust in."

*Yes, life's fragile, but there's something you're not telling me. And I could question you till dawn, and you still wouldn't reveal it.*

# Mick Savage

Tick Tack Jack Tullock didn't want to talk about the old days.

"That was then and this is now," he said to Mick on the phone. "I'm a successful rancher, got a place in the community. Even got a family. No way I'm lettin' it come out what I was back then. Besides, this Gaby chick you say was tryin' to reform me, I don't hardly remember her. And this Darcy guy, not at all."

"But you did know Laura Mercer. Lady Laura."

"Maybe. Well, yeah. But all that was over years ago. I can't risk it comin' out."

"Nothing's going to 'come out,'" Mick said patiently. "My questions are only for background on an unrelated case."

"Well, if it's unrelated, why d'you need to ask them?"

Good point. Frankly, Mick wasn't convinced that poking

around in the DeLucci murder was getting them closer to finding Darcy. Maybe Darcy had read about the case and visited Gaby's grave out of morbid curiosity. Maybe he was on a self-guided tour of California cemeteries. Maybe he was just plain crazy.

The latter was the best explanation. And the best solution to the problem was to turn it all over to the SFPD and let them find him and his motives. But, no, Shar had to protect the freak....

He said to Tick Tack Jack, "Mr. Tullock, it's my assignment to ask these questions. If you'd like to speak with my employer—"

"I don't want to speak to *nobody*. I got a life here to protect. I got a rep-*u*-tayshun."

Mick suppressed a sigh. "I can have our lawyers draw up a document of confidentiality—"

" 'Confidentiality.' One of those words that don't mean shit these days."

A new tack occurred to Mick. "Well, Mr. Tullock, if you're so concerned with protecting your reputation, your involvement with the DeLucci murder must be serious. Something you didn't tell the police?"

"I never—"

"Something to hide?"

Long pause. "I never talked to the cops. They didn't know about me and Gaby."

Mick waited.

"Thing is...I can't do this over the phone. How do I know you ain't tapin' it?"

"I'm not. But if you'd prefer to talk in person, I can come there."

"To my ranch? No freakin' way!"

"You're west of Portland, right?"

"Yeah. So?"

"I could meet you any place you wish."

"Determined, ain't you?"

"Yes, sir, I am."

Another pause, longer this time. "Well, if you bring along that document you talked about... You know where McMinnville is?"

"I can find it."

"Okay, I got a place there where I can meet you. I'll tell you the address and phone number. You call when whatever flight you catch gets in, and I'll give you directions. In a way, it'll be good to get this off my chest. Real good."

# Darcy Blackhawk

*What happened to you?*

He was standing in an alley between two apartment houses across from the little brown girl's building, but she hadn't come out or gone in. She was his only friend in this city—maybe in the world—but he couldn't make himself climb the steep marble steps and ring the bell. He was going to have to run away from there, just like he'd run away from Shar's last night. And then where would he go and what would he do?

No place.

Nothing.

When had the world gotten so scary?

There was a time when he was happy and safe, with Mom and Dad and Robbie in the big house in Boise. They'd been a regular family, not like the perfect ones you'd see on TV, but they'd gotten along. Mom and Dad were busy with their work, but they'd still had pizza nights and gone on camping trips. He'd graduated high school after flunking a few courses and having to go to summer school. Had gotten good with video cams, even had a job for a while editing for a TV station. But then Dad died and he started drifting and drugging and now all the memories were scrambled.

Mom and Robbie would say it was the drugs, but he wasn't so sure of that. It might be like a disease in him, or maybe not. He wasn't sure of a damn thing.

He took one of the red-white-and-blue straws that he'd found in his pocket and started twisting it. It made him feel better, like his feet were solid on the ground. He'd grabbed a handful of the straws... when? Where? Didn't matter, they helped him get through.

Somebody went up the steps of the house across the street. Not the little brown girl. Taller woman, no cape. She put a key into the lock and disappeared inside. A little later lights went on in the top-floor windows.

A roommate? Last night he'd heard voices, music....

A couple came along the street, a little dog on a lead. Darcy pulled farther back into the shadows between the two houses. Couldn't stay there long. Couldn't go back to Shar's—he'd forgotten how to get there. The park again? Under that bush? His cozy shack on the river?

The river. So long ago, like a dream. Had he really ever been there?

Yes. He'd had friends there, a life. Sort of. But then the cops had rousted them and they'd run west till they hit the coast. South to... where was he now?

San Francisco. Remember: San Francisco.

What had happened then?

*What happened to you?*

# Sharon McCone

When I got back to M&M's I knew that Jimmy Crow's watch was working: he showed up exactly at eight. Shaggy dark blond hair, stubbly chin, dressed in faded jeans and a leather jacket so old that the elbows were cracked and peeling. He slouched onto a stool near the middle of the bar, and the bartender automatically placed a shot of whiskey and a beer in front of him. After he'd downed the shot Mario said, "Lady wants to buy you a drink," and nodded in my direction.

Crow turned and squinted at me with one eye. The other appeared to be swollen shut. "Lady, huh? In this place?"

I slid over toward him. "My old neighborhood hangout."

"Must've been years ago. Don't remember seeing you before."

I signaled to Mario to bring him another shot. "A few

years, yes. I used to live up on Guerrero. The building's gone now, everything's changed."

"You can say that again."

"There was a guy used to play here. Blues guitarist, name of Chuck Bosworth."

"Chuckie? Yeah, I know him. Still comes around sometimes, but he ain't the same no more neither. Had a stroke, can't play or sing worth shit. Calls himself the Nobody. What kind of a name is that?"

"A pretty sad one. You know where I can find him?"

Crow's one open eye took on a wily glint. "Why?"

I gave him my card. "The musicians' union hired me. Bosworth may be in line for some insurance money."

He peered at the card. "Didn't know he belonged to no union. Course, I don't know much about him. Just another barfly. You say there's money involved?"

"Some."

"How much for me if I take you to him?"

I studied him, gauging his price. Decided it wasn't very high. "Twenty dollars."

"Done." He held out his hand.

"When we get there."

He'd expected that response and didn't look disappointed, just said for form's sake, "You drive a hard bargain, lady."

He didn't know the half of it.

The neighborhood where Jimmy Crow directed me— Visitacion Valley—is one of the worst in the city, and the alley he led me down was unlighted and smelled of garbage and urine. Nearby on a rise near McLaren Park loomed the infamous Sunnydale Housing Projects, World

War Two barracks converted to apartments that once were extolled as an excellent example of public housing, but have now degenerated into squalor, violence, and all too often death.

Gangs patrol the bleak landscape, dealing drugs or extorting money from the hard-pressed residents. Stores have bulletproof windows, barred doors, and turnstiles, surveillance cameras, and armed clerks. Drive-by shootings happen weekly, and burglaries are a near-normal occurrence. The surrounding small dwellings mirror the projects: boarded windows, trash and broken glass in the yards, dead automobiles and trucks in the cracked driveways.

Who's to blame? The housing authority? The mayor? The residents themselves?

Nobody, maybe. It exists, that's all, as similar pockets of poverty do in every city in the country.

Jimmy Crow stopped and touched my forearm. "That's the place."

All I could see was a structure that looked like a falling-down chicken house.

"Where's my money?" he asked.

"Stays with me, until I talk with Bosworth."

"You said—"

"I know what I said. Don't push me." I was looking into the darkness, identifying shapes and alert for sounds that might mean danger.

"But you *said*..." He was whining now.

My hand went to my .357 Magnum, where it rested in the outside pocket of my bag. I'd removed it from the office safe tonight and brought it along—and a good thing. Armed was the only way I would've come into this area with a stranger, day or night.

I showed the gun to Jimmy Crow. He didn't look surprised, just shrugged and moved forward up a flight of rickety steps. I followed.

"Chuckie?" he called softly. "Chuckie?"

Over on Sunnydale a siren began wailing. Somewhere closer a woman screamed just once and then was quiet. A heavy, cold wind had come up, rustling trash around my ankles. There was a distant report from the projects that might have been a gunshot.

"Chuckie?"

Silence within the ramshackle structure.

Crow opened the door, and it nearly came off its hinges. The air that rushed out was fetid: old food smells, unwashed clothing, more garbage, urine and feces.

Crow said, "Chuckie don't have no lights or plumbing. When he's not here kids come in and crap and piss the place up." He moved inside and flicked a cigarette lighter, put its flame to a candle that stood on an oilcloth-covered table.

I'd seen squalor over the course of my career, but this was the worst. Two rooms, the door to the second hung with a bead curtain minus most of the beads. Heaps of trash in the corners of the front room, decaying food and armies of ants on paper plates, a single armchair, the fabric torn and bleeding its stuffing. The other room contained a filthy mattress topped by a twisted, equally filthy quilt. The floor was covered with dirty laundry.

"Jesus," I murmured.

"Pretty bad, huh?" Crow said. "The damned fool's so far gone he ain't got the sense to get himself on public assistance. Me, I got a nice gig days taking care of this sick old man in the lower Mission. One of these days he'll kick, leave me all his money."

Crow was starting to annoy me. "Wait outside," I told him.

"My money—"

"When I come out."

He retreated.

Trespassing, illegal search. Yes, but who was going to press charges? Not the Nobody.

I moved slowly through the shack, inspecting everything. On the table: grocery bag containing a couple of tins of sardines; empty malt liquor bottle; crumpled cigarette pack and a tuna fish can full of ashes and butts. Under the chair's cushions: a racing form from 2007, three pennies, a ballpoint pen from someplace called Leo's Club, and a broken guitar pick. In the bedroom: nothing in any of the pockets of the strewn clothing, but when I lifted the thin mattress I found a five-by-seven clasp envelope. I opened it; the only thing inside was a photograph.

A tall, thin man with a gaunt, wasted face; a brown-haired woman, her head thrown back in laughter so you couldn't really make out her features; a black man with a guitar clutched against his chest, as if he didn't know what to do with it; and another white woman, smiling directly into the camera's lens.

Gaby DeLucci.

I turned the photograph over. On the back someone—Bosworth, probably—had written on it in faded blue felt-tip: "The Four Musketeers."

I paid off Crow and waited alone for Bosworth's return, opting to sit on the bare, littered ground behind the shack's steps rather than breathe the fetid air inside. As the hours passed one part of me remained alert, registering sound, motion, and the swiftly dropping temperature. The other part slid into the almost trancelike state that makes a long surveillance possible.

What thoughts I had were of the photograph I'd found and the notation on its back: "The Four Musketeers." Gaby DeLucci, Chuck Bosworth, another man, and another woman. I supposed that the other man was Jack Tullock, aka Tick Tack Jack; the brown-haired woman must be Laura Mercer, aka Lady Laura. Gaby had supposedly been mentoring them, yet the photo and the inscription indicated a more egalitarian relationship. I wondered if—

A noise came from below: someone moving on the hard-packed earth.

I tensed. More sounds, low grunting voices, indicating that more than one person was coming uphill. I stood quickly, gripping my .357 in both hands, straining to hear.

A hurt, fearful cry, the words unintelligible. Then—no doubt this time—the sudden crack of a handgun firing not far away.

I drew farther back into the shadows beside the shack. The hillside was silent, except for a distant siren and the far-off grumbling of traffic. As if every living thing in the vicinity were holding its breath. The stillness seemed to last a long time. Then small creatures began to stir again, a man hooted somewhere below, voices rose up above. But no one came to investigate the shot. Rule of the urban jungle: stick to your own lair.

After a while I took out my small flashlight, moved carefully away from the shack. Everything seemed to be as before—rocks, thickets of dead weeds, refuse. I started down the slope, moving the light ahead of me. After a few steps it picked out a heap of rags on the littered ground—

No, not rags, a person.

Noises again, the rustling of some kind of shrubbery off to my left. I turned in that direction—almost too late. If I hadn't gone into a crouch and switched off the flashlight when I turned, it would've been.

The bullet whined damn close to my ear as it was. I saw the muzzle flash, heard the crack of the shot, as I flung myself to the ground. The second bullet whanged off rock to my left, not as close.

There was no time to set myself and return the fire. All I could do was scramble away downhill as fast as I could. A piece of broken glass sliced into the heel of my right hand, bringing a sharp stab of pain, but I managed to hang on to the Magnum.

A third shot. This one didn't seem to come anywhere close.

The ground dipped sharply and I rolled over and down into a weed-choked hollow. My momentum checked, I twisted around and scrubbed my eyes clear with my left hand, bringing the .357 up into firing position.

Nothing to see but darkness.

Silence for several seconds, then the faint sounds of movement. But not toward where I lay—away from it along the hillside. The sounds faded and silence resettled again, still thick and charged even though I sensed the shooter was gone. Either he thought one of his last two shots had hit me, or he was afraid he'd missed, seen that I was armed, and didn't want anything to do with a firefight.

I stayed put anyway, letting my pulse rate slow and getting my breathing under control. My palm hurt where the glass had cut it and it was still bleeding. I wiped off as much of the blood as I could, then tore a piece off the bottom of my blouse and wrapped it around the hand.

It didn't take long after that for the reaction to set in—a couple of minutes of dry-mouthed shakiness, and a shudder when I thought of how close those first two bullets had come to ending my life. This would have been a hell of a place to die.

After maybe fifteen minutes I crawled out of the hollow and climbed the slope to where I'd seen the raggedly dressed body. It still lay in the same spot, motionless. I'd lost my flashlight at some point, so I had to kneel down close to see that it was a man lying prone with his arms along his sides. Long gray dreadlocks spread out over his shoulders.

With some difficulty I turned him over. There was a black stain of blood across the front of his filthy shirt. I was pretty sure I knew who he was, but I put my face close to his to make sure. Right, dammit—the black man in the photograph, Chuck Bosworth, the Nobody. His face was a mass of cuts and bruises, as if he'd recently been beaten.

But he was still alive. Barely, his breathing labored, his pulse thready.

My cell phone still worked—small miracle, after that tumbling scramble downhill. I switched it on and called 911.

# THURSDAY, SEPTEMBER 9

# Mick Savage

The road across southwestern Oregon was mostly flat and straight, with pine-topped hills in the distance. Once he'd left behind the clutter of strip malls and fast-food joints, more pines and trees heavy with some kind of nut closed in to either side of the asphalt. Fruit stands edged the highway. He slowed as he passed through small towns where people moved lazily along the sidewalks, calling out greetings to one another; some even waved at him. Nobody was in a hurry—it was too fine a morning for that.

Mick had caught a flight to Portland at the obscene hour of six that morning and now, at a little after eight, he was sucking down coffee from a Styrofoam cup in order to stay awake. Before he'd exited the airport in his rental car he'd phoned the number Jack Tullock had given him; the woman who'd answered said Tullock wasn't there yet, Mick should come on over anyway.

Tick Tack Jack. Jesus, it sounded like a breath mint.

McMinnville turned out to be an attractive small city in the Willamette Valley wine country. Mick recalled that his late Uncle Joey had once worked in a restaurant there. A few blocks off Third Street, the main drag, in a section of small, well-kept homes, he located the address Tullock had given him, a small frame cottage painted pale blue and surrounded by rosebushes.

The woman who came to the door was a few years older than Mick, with upswept dark hair and gold-rimmed glasses that perched on the tip of a kind of skimpy nose. She wore a pink-and-white waitress uniform with her name—Rosa—stenciled over the blouse pocket.

"Jack's still not here," she said. "I can't imagine what's keeping him, but I have to get to work."

"I can wait in my car for him, if it won't make your neighbors uneasy."

"Not at all. This town's pretty laid back."

Back in the rental car he called Shar and reported his whereabouts.

"Okay," she said. "You get a line on Laura Mercer?"

"Her former employers are vacationing in the Greek Isles, the maid told me. I sent them a message, but haven't heard back yet."

"Well, I located Chuck Bosworth. Somebody shot him last night in front of his shack in Visitacion Valley. He also looked like he'd recently been beaten. He's in critical condition at SF General."

"He going to pull through?"

"The doctors aren't sure yet. Let me know what you find out from Tullock."

Mick put in another call to the offices of Merrill Lynch

in San Francisco's financial district, where his current love, Alison Lawton, worked as a broker. "Guess where I am."

"Not at home; I just tried to call you."

"McMinnville, Oregon."

"What for?"

"Case. I'm probably coming back later. You want to have dinner tonight?"

A pause. "Mick, you've broken three of our dinner dates in the past few weeks. I know your job's demanding, but I can't keep setting myself up for disappointment."

Ominous old story. His last serious love interest, Charlotte Keim, had acquired a fiancé while he was caught up in an investigation.

Alison added, "I've got a meeting. Call me when you get in."

He closed his phone and brooded, picturing Alison. Tall, willowy blonde, and to his eyes beautiful. Funny, smart, and genuine. He'd met her when they were both buying men's socks at Macy's; her big feet didn't bother him, though she considered them a major detraction. They'd been together since last winter, and he'd thought everything was going fine—until now.

Maybe he should quit the agency. He and Derek Ford were making great money from SavageFor.com. Derek had been making noises about leaving recently; even though his was largely a desk job, he felt it was getting in the way of his real life, which consisted of making the rounds of the clubs and meeting women. Derek wasn't lazy; he worked hard when motivated, but it took something major to do the motivating. He'd busted his butt developing SavageFor.com, but now it was managed by one of the Internet giants, and he and Mick had little to do with it except cash their checks.

Mick supposed the two of them could go off on their own and create other sites, but he knew deep down that wasn't going to happen. Derek was at a stage in his life when he wanted to play and, besides, Mick liked investigative work. The tech stuff was fun, but at the end of the day he needed to feel that he'd done something to make a difference for somebody. Too much like his father, he supposed. Ricky could've sat down and never worked a day for the rest of his life, but instead he was arranging exhausting nationwide tours for charity.

*Stuck with a work ethic, dammit.*

More time limped along.

Getting late. He scanned the street in his side-view mirror, saw a woman walking with a familiar bouncy gait. Rosa, returning from work. He met her on the sidewalk.

She blinked. "You still here?"

"Yeah. Jack never showed."

"What?" Her eyes filled with alarm.

"I've been here all day."

"Oh, God! Something's happened to him!"

"Maybe he just got sidetracked. I tried his cell a couple of times, but it was out of service."

"No, no, no! He's been hurt—or worse."

"Why d'you say that?"

"Because I've always known he had something to hide about his past and now I'm afraid it's caught up with him."

# Sharon McCone

I'd spent the early part of the morning answering questions about Chuck Bosworth at the SFPD. I gave them a carefully edited story: I was investigating the Gaby DeLucci murder in hopes of gathering information for a true-crime book. No, I did not have a client—not quite a lie, but I couldn't tell them I was acting on my own behalf.

"You must not have much business coming your way lately." Inspector Devlin Fast was a large black man with a bald head, horn-rimmed glasses, and a short gray beard. His brown suit was rumpled, and when he spoke he revealed crooked yellow teeth. In spite of those visual defects, he exuded an air of confidence.

"Actually, we have so much that I feel free to indulge my interests on the side."

He gave me a skeptical look, but simply said he'd be in touch.

*     *     *

The rest of the morning was frustrating because I'd had too little sleep. My hand hurt where I'd sliced it on the broken glass. Ted popped into my office to show off a colorful array of new silk shirts that had just arrived by UPS, proclaiming the fabric to be his fashion statement for life. When I snapped at him, citing his Western, Hawaiian, grunge, Edwardian, and numerous other phases, he blinked in hurt and shut himself in his office. I felt like such an ogre that I made amends by coaxing him out of there and taking him to lunch at Gordon Biersch, where I succumbed to ordering a Hop Stoopid Ale and paid for the indulgence—as its name had implied I would—by spending the afternoon feeling logy.

Ricky called at two: yesterday I'd asked him to find out whatever he could about Chuck Bosworth's current life, but none of his contacts knew anything. Around three Will Camphouse called from Tucson, in response to my request about the Moccasin Telegraph. There was nothing out there regarding Darcy.

After that I talked with Saskia, and she told me she'd had a long conversation with my other mother. The two of them had liked each other instantly when they met at Hy's and my wedding reception—in spite of Darcy's nearly burning the garage down—and Ma knew what it was like to lose a son to wandering. My brother Joey had disappeared in his late teens and moved around the country for years, leaving only a trail of postcards to Ma as indications of his whereabouts until he overdosed up in Eureka.

Ma had seen a lot of loss in her day, but I think it was Joey's death that really haunted her. Thoughts that it was somehow her fault that he was damaged occurred daily; regrets over what she might've done to save him nagged at her; worse was the secret, guilty feeling that he'd done us all a favor. My birth mother would face the same if Darcy never returned, or died.

She said, "Nobody's heard from him? Or anything about him?"

"Not since he ran away from my house the other night. Tell me, did he ever mention the name Gabriella DeLucci to you?"

". . . No, not that I recall."

"What about Tick Tack Jack, Lady Laura, or the Nobody?"

"I'd remember if I'd heard those names. What are they, rock groups?"

"Nicknames of Jack Tullock, Laura Mercer, and Chuck Bosworth."

"I don't know any of those either."

I sighed. "I can't understand why Darcy hasn't tried to contact me again. Unless the trouble he was in caught up with him, or he's gone to ground somewhere."

Saskia was silent.

I read her thoughts. "If you're brooding about having been a bad mother to him, don't. You raised Robbie exactly the same way and look how she's turned out."

"I can't help but feel I did something wrong. I should have tried harder with him, or foreseen that a situation like this was coming. I knew the signs, but I just didn't want to acknowledge them—"

"Stop!"

". . . So what will you do now?"

"Find a new lead. Find Darcy."

I checked with SF General before leaving the pier for an appointment at Glenn Solomon's office late that afternoon: I was told that Chuck Bosworth had died at three-seventeen without regaining consciousness. His system hadn't been strong enough to counteract the effects of the beating and the bullet that had ripped through his chest close to his heart. The Nobody was really nobody now.

They asked me if I knew his next of kin. No, I said, I didn't. After I hung up, I wondered if the city still had a potter's field and, if so, where it was.

When I had inquired earlier that afternoon, Glenn Solomon told me he had not been Gaby DeLucci's attorney, but that he and her father had roomed together during college, and that when Gaby called him for an appointment he'd scheduled one for a few days after she died. I scheduled one for late that day.

Glenn leaned back in his desk chair, hands resting on his considerable corporation. Even at the end of a working day his mane of white hair was perfectly groomed, his elegant gray suit unwrinkled. I sat across from him in my jeans and sweater, feeling unkempt. His posh suite of offices on the thirtieth floor of Three Embarcadero Center had recently been redecorated by his wife, interior designer Bette Silver, in tones of gray that conveyed both warmth and dignity. They made me feel unkempt too.

"Attorney-client confidentiality," he said, "extends beyond the client's death. However, my friend, inasmuch as you're acting in Gaby DeLucci's best interests, and of those of us who cared about her, I'll waive the privilege."

It was so like Glenn to emphasize what a favor he was

doing me, but I could forgive him. He was one of the most influential attorneys in the city, yet he'd always treated me as an equal, done me many such favors, and welcomed me into his home. When he called you "my friend," Glenn meant it.

"The changes Gaby was thinking of making," he went on. "I consulted the file to see if she'd gone into them specifically on the phone. She had not."

"And you didn't press her about them?"

"I asked, she declined. She promised to tell me about them when we met, but she was killed before our appointment."

"Did she tell you she'd spoken about them with Clarence Drew?"

"No, but I assumed she might have wanted to remove him as trustee. Drew exerted a great deal of control over Gaby, and once she turned eighteen she most likely wanted him out of her life."

"What sort of control?"

An odd look came over Glenn's face, and I felt attorney-client privilege closing in. "Financial, of course. As trustee he governed how much she could receive from the trust and how she could spend it."

"And besides that?"

"You know, you have an annoying way of digging under the surface of the facts."

I waited.

"Very annoying." Glenn closed his eyes, seeming to meditate on my question. Then he sighed. "But I suppose some truths must be revealed. Since Gaby was thirteen, I suspected Drew had been having sexual relations with her."

"Jesus! What made you think that?"

"The way they interacted—looks, actions, body language. I'm not the only one who felt that was what was going on. But no one had any proof."

"Why didn't she—"

"Do anything about it? I don't know. I should have approached her, tried harder to gain her confidence, but in my position..." He shook his head.

"Why didn't you go to the authorities?"

"Again, no proof. One thing I did do was to monitor Drew carefully through the years, and I've seen no indication of fiscal indiscretion in regard to the trust. He lives as he always has, even after his wife died a year ago."

"What did the wife die of?"

"Heart failure. Nothing sinister."

"You said you suspected sexual abuse because of the way they interacted. Can you be more specific?"

"She seemed alternately afraid of him and as though she held the power in the relationship. Her body language was conflicted: sometimes she cringed from him like an abused puppy; other times she was seductive, aggressive."

"Do you think Drew's wife knew?"

"They usually do. And look the other way."

"Is there anyone Gaby might have confided in about the molestation?"

"Possibly, but I don't know much about her private life."

My phone rang. Rae, returning an earlier call I'd placed to her.

"I've got to take this," I said to Glenn, "and you need to go home. I've used up enough of your time."

"Gladly," he told me, standing up and stretching. For

Glenn, stretching involved raising his arms halfway to shoulder level.

"Your neighbors—Lucy and Park Bellassis. Do you know them?" I asked Rae as Glenn shrugged into an overcoat and left his office.

"Not very well. We had them over for drinks once, and they reciprocated."

"Is that well enough to ask them over for cocktails on short notice?"

"...I suppose so. But why?"

"That case Mick and I are working. I need to see them in an informal setting."

"Well, okay. I'll see what I can set up."

Five minutes later she called back. "The Bellassises are coming. Get your butt here. Mrs. Wellcome and I will be deep in preparations and will need all the help we can get."

# Darcy Blackhawk

*The night is different....*

Scarier, because he didn't know what might be coming at him from the dark. But safer, because he could hide more easily.

He moved along the street, slipping between buildings or down stairwells if somebody looked funny at him. There was a café with outdoor tables; on one of them a customer had left a few dollars as a tip. He took the bills, walked a block or so, and bought himself a sweet roll and some coffee. Sugar, that kept you awake.

He wasn't a thief, he was through with that. He needed the food to survive.

He downed his meal, licked his sticky fingers, finished the coffee. Looked for a bin and threw the trash into it. Protect the Earth, Saskia was always telling him. If he did, the land would nurture him.

Indian bullshit. The only thing being Indian had done for him was get him sneered at on the street.

Here, though, nobody sneered. He moved among them like he belonged. But it was getting cold. He'd better think of someplace to sleep.

*The night is different....*

# Mick Savage

Jack Tullock's ranch was a long way down a two-lane highway that curved gently through farmland. Dark out there, headlights sweeping empty barbed-wire-fenced land. Occasional lights flickered from buildings in the distance. The road to the ranch lay on their left, spanned by a tall gate emblazoned with its name like you'd see in an old Western. He turned in, following Rosa's taillights.

He'd learned from her that she was Tullock's daughter from an early marriage. Tullock had left her mother when she was a baby, but returned to Oregon years later, after he'd kicked his drug habit. Now he and Rosa were friends, had breakfast most mornings when Tullock drove into McMinnville for his Narcotics Anonymous meetings.

The taillights led him along a bumpy ranch road; the rental car was low-slung and didn't take the ruts very well. The branches of a windbreak of sturdy pines moved restlessly against the cloudy sky. Eerie rattling cries filled the air as he passed a fenced enclosure.

The outline of a house appeared before them. Old-fashioned wood frame with dormer windows, not a glimmer of light in the place. As the headlamps swept over it, Mick saw that it was in poor repair and needed painting.

He stopped the car and got out, Rosa joining him. He asked her about the strange rattling sounds.

"Pheasants," Rosa said. "Jack raises them. Also llamas and ostriches. There's even a camel in the corral behind the barn. No cattle, sheep, or horses. My father likes the exotic."

"Aren't camels mean?"

"Yes. They spit. Llamas aren't much better."

Tick Tack Jack was sounding weirder and weirder.

The only sounds were the creaking of the boards as they went up the front steps. Rosa knocked a couple of times, then Mick pounded loudly. No response from within.

He looked down at her, saw that her face was tense and still. She reached out tentatively and touched the handle; it turned and she nudged the door open, calling out and feeling for a light switch on the inside wall. Only echoes of her own voice answered her.

Mick held her back and squeezed inside ahead of her. Rag rugs, old oak furniture, watercolors of flowers on the walls. Everything neat and seemingly in its place.

"They should be here," Rosa said.

He looked to the right. Formal parlor with velvet and needlepoint-covered furniture. Nobody in his right mind would sit there. The room across the hall was filled with exercise equipment. Kitchen behind it and den at the back. No signs of anything out of the ordinary.

Rosa led him upstairs. Three bedrooms, full bath. Beds unmade, toys scattered on the floor of the two smaller rooms.

"It's not like them to have it this messy," Rosa said. "Beth's compulsive about housekeeping."

Mick went into the bathroom. The toothbrush holder was empty, but there was shampoo and conditioner in the shower stall. A safety razor and shaving cream sat on a shelf above the sink, and a damp towel was draped over the toilet.

Rosa called to him from the master bedroom. "There're gaps on the clothes poles, but it looks like most of their stuff is still here."

He joined her. Western shirts, jeans. Work boots and athletic shoes. Costume jewelry in a box on the dresser. A leather-bound Bible on the bedside table. He picked it up.

"Is your father religious?" he asked.

"In his way. A belief in a higher power is important to the twelve-step process."

The pages flopped open randomly, as if they'd been turned many times. He put the Bible down, followed Rosa from the room. Only one thing was certain: Jack Tullock and his family had left, taking few—if any—of their possessions, not even his well-worn Bible.

# Sharon McCone

As I drove to Rae's, the feeling that Lucy Bellassis had withheld something the previous day kept nagging at me. Maybe it was related to Gaby's murder, maybe not; talking with Lucy again, getting a look at Park, seeing the two of them together might help me find out. I was glad Rae had agreed to issue the invitation for cocktails to the Bellassises, and it was the perfect night for it: Ricky wasn't due back till the morning, but when he arrived he'd be tired and want peace and quiet till his younger children descended on him for the weekend.

Peace and quiet. I'd craved those qualities more and more since I'd been released from rehab. Care centers—no matter how nice—are busy and noisy. There're always people in the hallways, nurses and orderlies coming into your room in the middle of the night and waking you up to give you a pill—or to see if you're asleep. They have posted visiting hours, but that's because the state requires it; nobody observes them. You might as well be in bed at a major intersection.

But I resented the demands of my yearnings, felt stirrings inside me. The familiar old stirrings craved action, the excitement of the chase and a fight.

*Selfishness*, I told myself. I had Hy, my families, my friends to consider.

*Be careful. Even if you hadn't been badly injured, you're no longer as resilient as you used to be.*

*Wisdom. Reap the benefits of hard-taught experience.*

*Bullshit*, I told myself.

If I didn't respond to those stirrings now, I'd only be living half a life.

Rae and Mrs. Wellcome were bustling around the kitchen, spearing bits of cheese and fruit and prosciutto with toothpicks and microwaving frozen canapés from Trader Joe's. I knew that Mrs. Wellcome despaired of Rae's entertaining skills and was constantly recommending caterers. Rae had tried a few of them, but found them overpriced and snootily obsequious. One had extravagantly padded his bills. Besides, she'd said to me, what was wrong with simple stuff?

Ricky had concurred. "In Bakersfield," he'd said, "Vienna sausage, tortilla chips, and Cheez Whiz are what get a party going."

The doorbell rang, and I signaled to Rae that I'd let the visitors in.

Park Bellassis was dark-haired, slim, and handsome in a prep-school way. He looked startled when I opened the door. "We must have the wrong house," he said.

"No, no," Lucy told him. "This is Sharon McCone, Ricky's sister-in-law. Remember?"

"Right." Park seemed somewhat tired and withdrawn, but came out of himself once drinks were served and said complimentary things about Ricky's music. Lucy chattered on as she had yesterday, but she seemed brittle and on edge as she explained to Park that my agency was investigating Gaby's murder. He became more attentive.

"Not for Clarence Drew?" he said. "I understand her death was the best thing that could've happened to him."

"Meaning he was left in control of a multimillion-dollar trust?"

"More like a billion, I've heard."

"But he hasn't abused his position."

"Drew's into power, not money. Controlling that trust puts him in a position to exert influence on a good many people."

"Politicians?"

"Among others." Bellassis didn't elaborate.

To break the silence I eyed the canapés and settled on a mushroom-and-cheese puff. "I am so hungry!" I said.

I wasn't, but tonight seemed suited to the casual, somewhat ditzy role I'd perfected while plumbing for information at numerous business interviews, lunches, cocktail parties, and formal dinners.

*Me? Oh, I just run this little agency. Mainly we trace deadbeat moms or dads. I got out of college and there wasn't much I could do with a BA in sociology, and investigative work was more interesting than sitting in classes for God knows how many years till I could get my PhD.*

The act was getting harder to pull off because I'd gotten my name and picture in the papers too many times, but

I wasn't all that sorry to have to tone it down. Sometimes I used to think: *God, what crap! Is this what the one and only life I possess is to be about? Children's games? Masquerades? Hide-and-seek? Charades?*

But recently I'd concluded that I was being too hard on myself. I might be playacting, but it was for high stakes—often the highest there are.

I grabbed another canapé and popped it into my mouth.

Park and Lucy seemed disarmed by my behavior. I saw Rae's smile as she came into the room and apologized for not greeting her guests. She'd told me many times that it amazed her what a chameleon I could be.

"So," I said to Park, "you're the head of Bellassis Aviation Services. You fly much?"

"Not as much as I'd like. Unfortunately, administrative duties take up most of my time."

"And you, Lucy, I believe you said you fly too?"

"Some. My license is current, but I prefer to limit myself to the right seat."

"My little copilot," Park said.

Irritation flashed in Lucy's eyes. "The right seat can be trickier than the left."

She was correct: it's where the flight instructor sits and some controls are reversed; if the pilot becomes confused, makes a mistake, or simply nods off, it takes skill to pull out of the situation.

"Well, I fly every chance *I* can get." I leaned forward and engaged Park in a discussion of airplanes, all the while watching Lucy's reactions.

She had become tight-lipped, and her gaze wandered through the room, coming to rest on a row of Ricky's gold records and Grammy awards.

Rae said to her, "Sometimes it's tough being married to such an overachiever."

"But you achieve too. I don't do anything."

Park's mouth twitched as he looked from me to his wife. "You do plenty of things. Your charity work—"

"Is not on a par with what another woman might have done to make you proud. You would've been better off married to Gaby." To Rae she added, "Park and Gaby were engaged at the time she died, did you know that?"

"Sweetie, we were *not* engaged—"

"Not formally, but you were fucking."

"Lucy, please!"

"Gaby was the love of Park's life."

"Lucy!"

She stood. "Now I've made an ass of myself. It's an old family tradition. But then, social blunders are harmless compared to the other stuff. I'd better leave." She fled from the room, snagged her fleece jacket from the hall tree, and was gone. I excused myself and went after her.

She was standing on the front steps, putting on her jacket. When I touched her arm she pulled away. "You don't need to make me feel better. I know I was out of line in there. But sometimes it all gets to be too much for me."

"What does?"

"The polite chitchat. The pretense that Park and I are a normal young couple."

"I wonder if such a thing exists. Actually, I followed you out because I want to show you something." I took the photograph I'd found in Chuck Bosworth's shack from my pocket and held it out to her. "Gaby's in the center, but do you know who the other people are?"

She turned it over, looked at the stamp and notation on the back. " 'The Four Musketeers'—Gaby, Chuck Bosworth...The others are probably Tick Tack Jack and Lady Laura. Where did you get this?"

"I found it with some old documents."

The answer seemed to satisfy her. She gazed intently at their faces.

"Who do you suppose took the picture?" I asked.

"I have no idea. Gaby told me that Jack was a photographer; he documented everything, from people to rocks and wildflowers. She said he could be annoying, always popping up with his camera and demanding they strike poses. Since Tullock's in this picture, maybe it was taken on a timing device." She hugged her elbows across her upper body. "Frankly, I hate to look at it."

"Why?"

"Because that summer was a bad time for me. Gaby and I had been best friends, but then she abandoned me for...those people. And then she came back and tried to act like nothing happened. But she was changed—hard and angry. We had an argument the morning of the day she died."

"About...?"

"You know, I can't remember. All I know is we parted on bad terms, and I've regretted it ever since. This picture—can you contact Jack Tullock and find out if he took it?"

"Yes. He owns a ranch near Amity, Oregon. The Jokin' Jack."

"Amity? Where's that?"

"In Yamhill County, a couple of hours from Portland."

"Maybe..."

"Yes?"

"Maybe he has others from that time that might tell more about Gaby's murder."

"We'll see."

Lucy hurried off home. When I went back inside, Park Bellassis said, "I don't know what's the matter with Lucy. She doesn't usually go off like that."

"No problem," I told him, and excused myself to go to the kitchen, where I almost banged the swinging door into Mrs. Wellcome's head. Her gray hair was pulled back from her forehead and secured in a knot at the nape of her neck; the style rendered her long, sharp-featured face stern. She'd been leaning forward, listening.

"Eavesdropping again, huh?" I said.

"That young woman is a bundle of nerves. If I were you and Ms. Kelleher, I'd watch her carefully."

Those of us who were frequent visitors to this house pretended we disapproved of Mrs. Wellcome's nosiness, but she knew that wasn't so. Actually both Rae and Ricky relied on her insights into the many guests who crossed the Kelleher/Savage threshold. Ricky had been known to consult with her many times about dubious visitors.

I asked Mrs. Wellcome, "What about the woman's husband?"

"More difficult to understand. He's uneasy around his wife, probably because he doesn't know what to expect next. The marriage is in trouble. Has been for some time now, unless I miss my guess."

"You got all of that listening at the door?"

"I've been keeping an eye on that couple for some time, ma'am."

"Cut out the 'ma'am' stuff. Have you ever considered going to work for my agency?"

"I'm perfectly happy where I am, but I could be persuaded to help out when domestic matters are involved."

*Lord help me, an aspiring private investigator is managing Rae's and Ricky's household.*

# Darcy Blackhawk

*How could you do this to me?*

He'd hidden in the park all last night and most of today, taking a few trips past the little brown girl's apartment building. Now it was dark again, he was back in the park, and he was hungry. He hadn't eaten since the sweet roll and coffee.

The little brown girl...

He tried to remember what they'd done after he met her. At one time she'd taken him to a restaurant and bought him a burger. A restaurant where the waiter didn't look at him like he was a freak. After that he didn't remember anything except for the steep steps of the big house and waking up in the girl's bed.

Why'd he leave? Oh, right—to go to Shar's. But he'd screwed that up, and now he had nobody.

Shar had abandoned him too. Hadn't e-mailed him

back. Where was his computer? He had a frantic moment, pawing the ground around him, then remembered he'd sold it someplace, sometime.

The river. Long, quiet days. And then Laura had come, disturbing them. And then they'd had to run anyway. And then she'd abandoned him too.

*How could you do this to me?*

# Sharon McCone

It was almost midnight, and I couldn't sleep. Finally I gave up trying and went to the kitchen. The table was littered with the usual stuff: junk mail, half-read books, unpaid bills, spare change, dry cleaners' tickets, my purse and briefcase. I shoved it all aside, booted up my laptop, and began clicking through sites containing the phrase "the four musketeers."

Nineteen-twenties silent film adaptation of the classic novel *The Three Musketeers* by Alexandre Dumas.

Nineteen-seventy-four Richard Lester film. Another film a year later, with Raquel Welch and Oliver Reed.

French quartet who'd dominated men's tennis in the 1920s and -thirties.

More movies. Scholarly works on the novel. Other movies loosely based on it with silly storylines.

What did this have to do with anything in the real world?

Musketeers: infantry soldiers dressed in plumed hats and capes, brandishing sabers.

Informal usage: comrades, friends. People who aid and support one another.

Four: Gaby, Chuck Bosworth, Laura Mercer, Jack Tullock.

Three: Laura Mercer, Chuck Bosworth, Jack Tullock.

Two: Chuck Bosworth, Jack Tullock.

One: Jack Tullock.

And now?

I tried to call Mick to find out what he'd learned from Tullock, but his cell was out of its service area.

Damn!

Okay, deep search. I wasn't as good at that as Mick, but I could try....

# FRIDAY, SEPTEMBER 10

# Darcy Blackhawk

*I love you....* she'd said.

She came to him out of the fog. The little brown girl.

She grabbed his arm. "Where the hell have you been?"

He tried to pull away; she was hurting him.

She yanked at him—hard. "Where did you go?"

"...No place."

"Bullshit! Who did you talk to?"

"...Nobody."

"God, you make me sick!"

She yanked again and started moving him along the street. She scared him, but he hadn't the strength to protest.

The drug haze was clearing, slowly. He lay flat on his back, eyes still closed. His tongue tasted like iron filings. He remembered the little brown girl shooting him up—when? His sense of time had left him.

Voices came from nearby.

A man. "...Shouldn't talk in here with him."

A woman. The girl. "I gave him a shot. He'll be out of it till morning. Besides, I don't want to talk upstairs where one of the nosy neighbors might hear us. The heating ducts in this place really transmit sound. Tell me what you did."

"Okay, I went to the house. You were right—he wasn't there."

"I told you he wouldn't be. I checked; he was at that bar association dinner."

"All right, all right. I'm sorry if I doubted you. Anyway, that house is huge and the grounds are damn dark in the fog."

Darcy could picture a house like that. In his mind, he moved closer to it.

"I went down the side, to the backyard where there's a little fountain. Man, Niagara Falls never sounded as loud as that trickle."

Darcy could hear the water. It pounded in his ears, and he wanted to run away from it.

"I found the junction box for the alarm. The connection was frayed—a snap to break it."

What was a junction box? Darcy wondered.

"Then I got in by busting one of the windows in the French doors."

Darcy heard the breaking glass.

"You broke the glass? That wasn't very smart. He'll know somebody was in there."

"What was I supposed to do?"

"Did you clean it up?"

"Hell, no! Wait till you hear the rest of this—you'll understand."

"I understand that you might've left fingerprints all over the place."

"D'you think I'm an idiot? I had gloves on. Anyway, there were DVDs and videos in the entertainment center. I went through them—nothing. The guy has weird taste."

Darcy pictured titles: *Night of the Lepus*; *Attack of the Crab Monsters*; *Jaws*; *Dracula*; *I Walked with a Zombie*. All favorites of his.

"I thought there might be more videos upstairs, so I went to the front hall, and then there was this noise. Snarling."

"God, a guard dog."

"No, a *little* dog. Like the movie stars are always carrying around in their purses. But it was a tough one; it came leaping at me, got hold of my pants leg, ripped it before I got away. I dropped one of *his* stupid twisties while I was doing it."

"Twisties?"

"Those straw things he's always making."

"What the hell were you doing with it?"

"They're all over the place here. I'd filled my pants pocket cleaning up after him, and one just fell out."

"And you left it there?"

"Why not? It points to him, not us."

Pause. "Maybe you're right. But you didn't get the tapes."

"No. Couldn't find them. If he's got copies there they're well hidden."

"Jesus!"

"Look, why don't we give it up? For all we know he's stashed them in a safety-deposit box."

"That kind of material? No, I don't think so. Besides, we've got *this* idiot on our hands, and he's seen our faces."

"So what do we do with *him*?"

"For now, keep him drugged up. Later, I don't know yet."

"Why don't you just let me beat it out of him?"

"Like you tried to do with Chuck Bosworth?"

Silence.

"We'll figure something out later. I have a couple of ideas...."

Darcy tried to move, but he felt paralyzed. How could she do this to him?

*I love you....* she'd said.

*I love you....*

# Mick Savage

After he and Rosa had finished searching Jack Tullock's house the night before, she'd left him there and driven home, asking him to call if her father returned.

Mick had suggested they call the police, but Rosa said no, Jack was "allergic" to them. He appropriated a big leather recliner and settled down to what he hoped would not be another long wait. The house was silent except for a clock that bonged on the quarter hour. Occasionally from outside he heard the eerie rattling cries of the pheasants. The last bong he was aware of was at three-thirty a.m. His eyelids grew heavy and he dozed....

Unfamiliar sounds brought him straight up in the chair, fully alert.

Stealthy movement outside, toward the back of the house. A creak. A scraping step. Then silence.

Mick got up and went quietly to the family room at the rear. Eased aside a corner of a curtain to peer out. Nothing to see but the dark shapes of outbuildings—a barn and a large prefab. No lights, no motion within the range of his vision.

He let the curtain fall back, feeling a shiver skitter along his spine. He'd been wanting to do fieldwork for a long time, but now he had to admit he was more comfortable as a techie. This was Shar's kind of thing— waiting in darkness, following people, having dangerous confrontations. And look where that had landed her last year: in a locked-in state from which nobody had ever expected her to return.

He'd see this situation through, but that would be it. Then strictly a desk jockey until he decided what he wanted to be when he grew up.

He went back along the hallway, his heart thumping, and let himself out the front door, cautiously followed the approximate path he judged the footsteps had taken. Skirted the barn looking for a window and came up against a high rail fence with a darkened security spot mounted on it. In the murkiness beyond two malevolent eyes glared at him; the face was tan and haughty; the lips pulled back showing large yellow teeth.

*Camel.*

The beast looked as if it was preparing to spit. Mick backed off. The camel snorted derisively. If a thought balloon had floated above its head, it would've said, "Cowardly human." It snorted again, then turned and plodded away to the other side of the corral.

Not Mick's idea of a pet. Nor were the llamas—wherever they were pastured. One of his friends had been bitten by a llama at a county fair and had the ragged scars to prove it.

He went back the way he'd come and this time noticed that the barn door was slightly ajar. He sidled up to it and peered inside. Total darkness and silence. Again he felt the shiver, but he girded himself and entered anyway. Took out his small flashlight and shone it around. Three stalls, empty. Bales of hay, neatly stacked. Tools arranged along the far wall. Workbench with an attached vise. Nothing else.

He moved outside and over to the prefab. It was more like a guesthouse than a shed, and wires—electric? phone?—extended to it from the house. No windows, and the door must be on the far side.

The ground here was covered with some kind of plant with burrs; the plants caught on the legs of his jeans, their long branches twining around his shoes. He made his way carefully to the rear of the prefab—and stopped just as light flashed on the opposite side and hurried footsteps slapped on the ground.

Mick was momentarily startled, then gave chase to a dark figure disappearing around the main house, but by the time he reached the top of the long driveway the person had started up a dark van that he hadn't noticed before and vanished down the road. Finally he retraced his steps to the prefab, whose door was open, spilling light.

Inside was a scene of chaos.

The building housed an office: metal desk; file cabinets; computer; fax machine; industrial-strength gray carpet; gray walls hung with framed documents. But the contents of the desk and cabinet drawers had been dumped on the floor and lay in a tumble of spilled files, manila envelopes, and photographs, scattered pens and pencils, invoices, and computer disks.

Mick squatted down and sifted through the mess. Pretty standard stuff: bank statements, feed bills, junk mail, catalogs. The bank statements showed that Jack Tullock was not on sturdy financial ground: he had only $267.30 in his checking account and $5,000 in a CD that wouldn't mature until next April; the bills, totaling roughly $1,500, were mostly unpaid. Mick examined the phone bill: Tullock had made two calls on Wednesday to the same number in San Francisco. He noted it.

He gathered up the envelopes full of photographs and then looked at the framed items on the walls: high school diploma; Future Farmers of America awards; topographical map of the area; aerial photograph that must be of the ranch; studio portrait of Rosa; ribbons from the Yamhill County and Oregon State fairs.

Next Mick went to the computer. Apparently Tullock wasn't all that concerned with others getting into his files; his password was stored. Mick clicked through the icons: bookkeeping; calendar; to-do lists. None of them had been added to in weeks. No documents stored on the hard drive. He clicked the e-mail icon: no new messages except for spam; no sent mail. The trash file was clogged—more of the usual catalogs and political plugs and fundraising pleas. A week-old reminder from Rosa that he'd scheduled a dentist appointment for after his NA meeting the following morning. A note from a fellow NA member called Marco asking if he'd come in early and help with setting up the coffee. Mick noted Marco's address. A one-liner from Tullock's wife telling him dinner was ready. Mick smiled; a lot of people he knew sent messages to each other from even closer proximity. Sometimes he e-mailed or texted Derek even though they were in the same office, seated a few feet away from each other.

He supposed whoever had ransacked the office could've deleted any messages that would give away his identity. If so, any deletions would still be on the hard drive. It was a widely held myth that deleting or double-deleting an item erased it for good; if you knew where and how to look, you could find its cyber footprint.

Mick went out to his rental to fetch his laptop. Linked the computers and began his search. Plenty buried on the hard drive, but nothing that had any significance for him. Whatever had spooked Tullock hadn't arrived electronically.

But something had spooked him—badly—and Mick's instincts told him it had to do with Gaby DeLucci's murder.

# Sharon McCone

I woke to light filtering through the kitchen windows, realized I'd fallen asleep on my computer keyboard. Put my hand to my cheek and felt the indentations from the keys on my skin. Jesus! What time was it?

The clock on the stove showed nearly ten. I'd wasted half of the morning.

I tried Mick's cellular number. It still wasn't working, but that could mean he was on a flight coming home. I hoped.

My dreams had been uneasy and confusing; my body was slick with the kind of sweat that comes from a bad night, and my muscles were cramped from sleeping in an odd position. I took a long hot shower, during which I planned for the day. Dressed and made a couple of appointments. Called Saskia to give her an update, but she was in court. Robin wasn't home. I had an urgent need to reach out to someone who would understand my love/hate feelings for Darcy.

Finally I dialed the wisest but frequently most inscrutable man I'd ever known—my birth father, Elwood Farmer.

"You are upset, Daughter."

Daughter! This from a man who on our first meeting wouldn't let me into his house until I'd "assembled my thoughts."

"Yes, I am. Have you ever met Saskia's son, Darcy?"

"No, I haven't had the displeasure."

"He's missing."

Silence.

"And she's asked me to locate him."

More silence. He was probably lighting a cigarette. I'd been trying to get him to quit, but he was stubborn about giving up an almost lifelong habit. When I spoke of the dangers of lung cancer he just shrugged or said, "Sooner or later something's gonna take me out."

"Elwood, I don't like Darcy!" I said.

"From what I understand of the young man, that's not an unusual reaction. But let me ask you this: do you have to like the persons you look for?"

"No, of course not. But this is complicated."

"Only because you allow it to be."

Now I was silent.

"Darcy is a pain in the ass. A boil on the butt of society." Elwood tells it like it is. Always. And often in terms that do not become a wise man.

"Unfortunately," he added, "he's also a boil on the butt of your mother. They are exceedingly painful to remove."

"And to sit on."

"True."

"So what is it you're telling me?"

"Don't you know?"

I was beginning to get his drift. I needed to separate the personal aspects of the case from the professional. I should search for my half brother as if he were a stranger a client had hired me to find.

"Thank you, Elwood."

"If you wish, you may call me Father."

After I broke the connection, I sat holding the phone, stunned. Since I'd discovered our blood relationship, we'd spent very little time together. He'd come to San Francisco only once, to visit me when I was in the Brandt Neurological Institute, and I'd had little chance to escape to Montana, a state I'd loved at first sight. But our relationship had strengthened over the miles, and now this exceedingly reserved man called me Daughter and had given me permission to call him Father.

Down the Peninsula to Palo Alto. My first stop there was at a nondescript stucco apartment complex on Alma Street near Stanford University—the type built to house students in the eighties. It was well kept up, with new paint and purple-and-white African daisies growing in raised beds in the courtyard around the small kidney-shaped pool. The manager, who had been listed in the phone book under the complex's name—Palm Grove—was Vincent George; he lived in a ground-floor unit off the arched entryway.

I'd called ahead, and Mr. George had readily agreed to see me. He remembered the tenants of apartment 215 well, due to the "unfortunate circumstances" of their leaving.

Now he served me a soft drink and led me into a fenced patio whose plantings mirrored those in the courtyard.

"Those girls," he said, deep lines crinkling at the corners of his eyes and mouth, "it was such a shame, with their whole lives ahead of them. Of course, the blond-haired one—what was her name?"

"Lucy Grant."

"Right. She wasn't killed, but she was damaged all the same. I'd see her coming home from her classes all hunched over and looking down at the ground, and it wasn't the weight of her backpack that caused it, but the death of her friend."

"How long did she stay on here?"

"Till the Christmas break. Then she was gone for good."

"Did she have any friends, frequent visitors?"

"Only the boy that Gabriella DeLucci had been seeing. Park, they called him—unusual name. He'd come around looking sad too, and sometimes they'd go out together. What happened to Lucy and Park?"

"She married him."

"Good." He nodded. "Good. They have each other for comfort."

*Or something*, I thought. I doubted either of them provided the other with much in the way of comfort, to say nothing of love.

"Gabriella and Lucy must've had other company. Women friends, perhaps?"

Mr. George frowned thoughtfully. "Lucy studied at the library a lot; at least every time I'd see her going out, she'd wave and call, 'I'm off to the library, Mr. G.' Gabriella was usually with Park."

"Do you remember anybody else who visited?"

He frowned, thinking. "Well, there were some people who turned up right after Gabriella moved in—two men and a woman. They asked what apartment she was in. I called her from my office to make sure it was all right to give them the information. You have to be so careful, these days....Anyhow, she told me no, asked me to say only her roommate was home. And I did—it's my job to protect the tenants."

"How did the people react?"

"Left quietly. Were more polite than I would've expected from the likes of them."

"What were they like?"

"Not quite, you know, clean. And poorly dressed."

"Can you describe them?"

"The woman had light brown hair. One man was white and young, looked like he'd had a hard life. The other man was black and quite a bit older."

"Anything else you can tell me?"

"I'm afraid not. Are you in touch with that girl—Lucy?"

"Yes, I am."

"Tell her hello for me. They were nice girls, both of them."

"I'll tell her, Mr. George."

Next stop, Peet's Coffee and Tea on Homer Street, a few blocks closer to the university, where I had arranged to meet with Will Smead, the faculty advisor to whom both Gaby and Lucy had been assigned.

Smead was a husky, balding man with horn-rimmed glasses, dressed in jeans and a T-shirt imprinted with

WORD POWER. He rose when I came up to his window table, asked what I would like to drink, and went to fetch my cappuccino.

"Now," he said when we were both seated, "what would you like to know about Gabriella DeLucci and Lucy Grant?"

I'd expected some cautiousness on his part, a request that I not name him as a source or involve him in a potential court case, but he seemed willing—even eager—to talk.

"You were their faculty advisor."

"Yes, both were majoring in English. My specialty is Shakespeare, with emphasis on the tragedies. It has been my experience that young, overprivileged women are particularly drawn to them, possibly because of a lack of tragedy in their own lives."

"Gaby DeLucci had experienced tragedy. Both her parents were killed in an accident when she was twelve, and she had no family."

He considered that, running his fingers around the rim of his coffee mug. "Yes, but I didn't sense that she'd experienced any real grief. She seemed...dissociated from her emotions."

One of the many documented responses to sexual abuse.

"Can you elaborate on that?"

"It's not easy to define. The girl lacked passion. In fact, sometimes she seemed almost automatonic. She could quote reams of Shakespeare, but without any genuine involvement. We put on an end-of-term production of *Othello*, and I mistakenly cast her as Desdemona— she was dull as a stump in the role. She didn't seem to have any friends except for Lucy Grant. During our initial—and only—consultation, I asked her about her aspirations, her dreams. She seemed genuinely puzzled by the question; all she said was, 'I never dream.'"

"Did she mean sleep-dream, or that she had no hopes for the future?"

Smead shrugged. "She didn't encourage me to pursue the subject."

"I've been told she had a boyfriend."

"I don't know about that, but I wouldn't doubt it, as attractive as she was."

"What about extracurricular activities? Charity work?"

He shook his head. "You have to understand that I had only the one conference with her, observed her in class for half of one term. She didn't reveal much about herself, was quiet and didn't relate."

"What about Lucy?"

"A normal, high-spirited individual. Unfortunately, she was having difficulty keeping up with her class work. She wasn't really Stanford material. If she hadn't left school voluntarily, I suspect she would have flunked out."

"How many conferences did you have with her?"

"Only the one. We'd scheduled another, but she canceled. Understandable, considering the circumstances. I was not surprised when she didn't return after the holidays."

"Back to Gabriella: you say she showed little emotion, and yet you cast her as Desdemona."

"Yes. I thought a meaty role would bring her out of her shell. Also there was something about her...a haunting or perhaps haunted quality that seemed perfect for a portrayal of that doomed woman."

He paused, seeming to listen to the echo of his words.

"I don't believe in extrasensory perception, but somehow I knew Gabriella DeLucci's life would be a short and unhappy one."

Since I had to drive right by SFO on my way back to the city, I decided to have a look at the Bellassis FBO. It would be a short detour and not time-consuming.

The FBO was a long, low building with big windows overlooking the general aviation tie-downs; tall palms grew close to it, casting their swaying shadows against the large slabs of white stone facing. I parked and entered a large lobby filled with overstuffed furnishings and decorated in soothing shades of blue—an ideal place for tired pilots to relax between long flights. A tall man in a white shirt with first officer's epaulets on its shoulders sprawled in one of the chairs, but otherwise the lounge was empty.

A woman in a blue uniform sat behind the reception desk, making entries into a computer. Before she noticed me, a man's agitated voice came from behind a partition.

"Dammit, Lee, I can't find the information on the Acme charter. D'you have it?" The man rounded the partition. Jeff Morgan.

He blinked at me, startled. "I know you. Aren't you Lucy's friend?"

"Yes, Sharon McCone."

"Right. Lucy's not here, and neither is Park."

"Actually, I just wanted to take a look around. I have a plane at Oakland, but I'm thinking of moving it to SFO. How about a tour?"

"Sure." Morgan turned to the receptionist. "See if you can find that information for me, and if Park comes in, ask him to join us."

We went outside. The wind was blowing heavily northeast to southwest, making takeoff and landing difficult for small planes and even the heavies. I looked up at Jeff Morgan: he was a handsome man, his blond hair tousled, his face deeply tanned. He would clean up nicely if he shaved the accumulation of stubble from his chin and put on something other than his scabrous flight jacket—worse by far than Hy's—and his dirty jeans.

"Actually," he said, "there's not much to see. Tie-downs here, hangars over there"—he motioned to our right—"and a smaller cluster of them to our left. Were you thinking of renting a hangar?"

"Probably."

"What kind of aircraft have you got?"

"Cessna 170B, fully restored."

"Nice." We were walking among the tethered planes now: Cessnas and Pipers, a couple of Citabrias, some homebuilts and small jets. "A plane like that deserves its own hangar."

"I'll need to see your rental price list."

"We've got them in the office."

"Have you worked here long?"

"Over two years."

"And you've been with Torrey all that time?"

"She was the one got me the job. We met at this bar we both like—Wildside in the city."

"Torrey fly?"

"Nah, she's temperamentally unsuited. Freezes up at the controls. She's okay as a passenger, though."

A voice called from behind us. "Yo, Jeff, Sharon!"

Park came jogging across the tie-downs. In his tailored blue suit, his hair well styled, he presented a marked contrast to his employee. "Lee says Jeff's giving you the grand tour."

"She's thinking of moving her plane to a hangar here," Morgan said.

"I was hoping I planted that notion in her mind the other night. Unfortunately, we don't have any free hangars just now."

"Put me on your waiting list," I said. "I'm in no hurry."

"Right at the top. Will you do that, Jeff? Now?"

He wanted to get rid of Morgan.

Jeff tugged an imaginary forelock. "Yes, master. See you, Sharon."

Park glared after him. "He's such a smartass. If it wasn't for Torrey and if he wasn't a good pilot, he'd be long gone."

I said, "How's Lucy today? I really enjoyed meeting her."

"Fit-throwing and all?"

"Oh, everybody pitches a wingding once in a while."

"Not you."

"You'd be surprised."

"I like being surprised."

He was moving too close to me, violating my comfort zone. I stepped away. "Park, it's good to see you again. I hope a hangar opens up soon. Got to get back to work now."

I left him standing next to a gleaming white-and-blue Piper, staring after me as if he wondered where his tentative pass had gone wrong.

Hy called at around two-thirty: the conference with the Swiss bankers had ended to his satisfaction; they'd agreed to honor RI's existing contract for executive protection. He'd be home late that night or early next morning.

"Can't wait to be with you, McCone."

"And me you, Ripinsky."

Mick phoned a while later, when I'd taken a break from my investigation to deal with some administrative duties and was in conference with Julia Rafael. Julia, a tall, haughty-looking Latina—who wasn't haughty at all—was my all-around general operative. Her somewhat severe features were softened by her wide brown eyes and flashing white smile. Today she was dressed casually in jeans and a tweedy sweater, her thick black hair in a ponytail. The cases she was working were mainly skips—deadbeat dads, missing moms, wandering teenagers.

Mick was still in McMinnville, he said, and explained about the Tullock family's disappearance. "The police are assuming it was voluntary but Tullock's daughter insists otherwise."

"What do you think?"

"Voluntary and hasty. I'd say they were running from someone. I checked a number down in the city that appeared twice on Tullock's phone bill; it's for M&M's Lounge."

"Trying to locate Chuck Bosworth."

"Right. The guy I talked to said he took a couple of calls for Bosworth after he left the night he was shot. The caller wouldn't leave a number or a message."

"Male?"

"Yep. Same voice both times."

"Probably Tullock, wanting to warn Bosworth to watch his back."

"Probably. He still hanging in there?"

"No, he died yesterday afternoon."

"Damn! There goes a lead."

"A human being too, Mick."

Before he could respond to the mild rebuke, I asked, "When are you coming back?"

"First flight I can book."

"Good. Check in with me when you arrive."

I broke the connection and looked at Julia. "What can you tell me about sexual abuse?" I asked her.

Startled look. "Plenty, of course, given my history. But why?"

I waved away the question. "Say the abuser is a man in his fifties, the victim barely in her teens when the abuse started. It's suspected in certain circles, but he's never been accused because the underage victim would deny it. If someone wants to warn others about the man, what recourse would she or he have?"

Julia, who had been abused by any number of men during her years as a teenage prostitute, looked thoughtful. "How long did it go on?"

"Five years or so. From age thirteen until the girl was killed at eighteen."

"Killed by her abuser?"

"Maybe."

"Well, if it was known to others who couldn't or wouldn't come forward because they had no evidence, there's a website they could contact: FreeToHarm.com. People report their suspicions and they put it out on the Net."

"That's potentially libelous."

"Yes, but normal laws don't apply much to the Net."

"True." Regulation of the rapidly growing twists and

turns of the Internet was as yet an unresolved issue. Hard to govern something that widespread and amorphous.

I swiveled to my keyboard, typed in "FreeToHarm .com."

The site came up: black letters on a Caltrans-orange background. I scanned its statement of purpose, then typed Clarence Drew's name in the box provided.

A page came up, complete with picture. The text read: "Suspected of having molested his legal ward from age 13 or 14, possibly longer. No other victims reported. Number of complainants: 5." Drew's addresses—both business and home—were given.

"This is pretty strong stuff," I said. "And possibly dangerous. None of it has been proven, unlike the sites that publicize the whereabouts of convicted molesters. Say you don't like your neighbor, so you put him and his address on this site. Somebody else has a vendetta against molesters and blows him away. And you, of course, are protected by anonymity."

"I admit it's over the top," Julia agreed. "But when there've been five complaints...well, you have to figure something was going on."

"Maybe."

"What were the dates on the posts?"

I clicked through them. "All within the past two weeks. Long after Gaby was dead."

FreeToHarm.com. Mick or Derek might be able to get information on who had made those posts.

# Darcy Blackhawk

*I couldn't've done that....*

He said the words aloud, staring at the newspaper story. The girl in the brown cape had just read it to him.

"The police think you did," she said. "They're already looking for you."

"How d'you know?"

"It says so in here."

They were in the dark bedroom in the tall house.

He sort of remembered another house. Dark too, and he'd gotten attacked by a stupid little dog. Or had that been just a story he'd heard someplace? He didn't think he'd been out of the house, had slept a lot, he guessed. Afternoon light was coming from around the dark burlap curtains.

The little brown girl showed him something else in the paper, a picture of the woman, young and smiling. Darcy knew her. Or did he? And how did he know she looked older now?

How? Where?

*The water running under the bridge. Her crazy laughter.*

Yes! The Salmon River. Lady Laura.

The places they'd stayed after they were sent away from there: none of them as nice, some really awful. But Lady Laura knew how to make them home. Last Thanksgiving she'd gone searching and found leftover fried chicken in a Dumpster behind a KFC, and they'd had a feast.

And now the girl was telling him Laura was dead.

*Her cold dead face...What I did...*

He lowered his face and stared numbly at his hands; they were dirty, the nails ragged.

Her voice hammered at him, asking the same questions that she had been all along.

"You knew her in Idaho, right?"

"...Yeah."

They'd been friends. Lady Laura was nice, shared her dope. Had that big, booming laugh that would send up echoes as they hunkered on the bridge supports above the shallow water.

"What did she give you to keep for her?"

That again. "Nothing."

"Sure she did."

"When?"

"Up in Idaho."

"Grass and meth. We used together. It's all gone."

"No, I mean something she wanted you to hold on to. Something valuable."

"I told you, I don't have anything valuable, not even my computer."

"Maybe you or Laura hid it someplace?"

"My computer?"

"Darcy, I don't know if you're very stupid or very crafty."

He had no opinion on that. A lot of people had called him stupid, but so far nobody had called him crafty. He wasn't even sure what "crafty" meant.

"Look," the girl said. "You were at the Salmon River with Lady Laura. Then the two of you came down here. Right?"

"Right."

"Tell me everything you remember about that time."

Remember. He'd forgotten so much. He looked again at the newspaper. He'd remember if he'd done it. Wouldn't he?

*I couldn't have done* that.

# Sharon McCone

I wanted to talk with Clarence Drew in person, but when I phoned his office the receptionist said he'd gone home for the day. No problem: I had his address on Filbert Street in Pacific Heights, and decided the shock value of having an investigator show up unannounced might catch him off guard.

Drew's block was an attractive one: shady elm trees, well-tended little front yards beyond low fences, Bay views between the detached houses. His lot was narrow—the standard San Francisco twenty-five feet—but the dwelling itself was a huge three-story Victorian.

I parked across the street but remained in my car for a moment, tapping my fingers on the steering wheel, considering my approach. My earlier conversation with him had not been adversarial, but a certain amount of pressure from me might elicit a more volatile—and truthful—response.

A uniformed maid with a cloud of black hair that dwarfed her small features answered the bell, looked skeptically at my credentials, then silently admitted me into a dark foyer; I glimpsed tapestries on the walls and a narrow staircase. She said in a slight Spanish accent, "I'll see if he's receiving visitors," and vanished.

I waited. The house was unnaturally quiet. No television sounds, no music, no one moving about. Eventually I heard footsteps coming down a back staircase—probably the maid returning. But then a door slammed at the rear.

I hurried along a hallway toward where the sound had come from into a spacious, well-appointed kitchen. Reached the outside door in time to see an old Chevy Camaro back down the driveway. The maid leaving—in a hurry.

I retraced my steps to the foyer. The house was silent again. I called out to Drew, received only echoes of my own voice in return.

Maybe he wasn't home. Maybe he'd sent the maid away because he didn't want to see me...no, he would have told her to get rid of me, not to run. Maybe he was hiding somewhere.

I had no business being here, even if I'd been let in by the maid, but my curiosity overwhelmed my good sense. I inspected the other ground-floor rooms. Formal parlor, with Hepplewhite furnishings that looked as if no one had ever sat on them, plenty of mahogany and a big, deep blue rug with raised pink flowers at each corner. Informal parlor, well used, with magazines, books, videotapes, and DVDs scattered about. Dining room, crystal and fine china displayed in cabinets and not a mote of dust on the gleaming table and sideboard. Tiled butler's pantry connecting to the kitchen: well stocked with canned goods, more dishes, linens, and flatware.

A low, whimpering sound came from one of the cabinets. I stooped down, saw its door was slightly open. Inside was a little dog with wide, frightened eyes; its body was quivering. I put out a hand to calm it, and it drew back its lips and snapped at me.

"Okay," I said. "You're scared. Stay in there."

The dog laid its head on its paws.

I left the kitchen and went back down the hallway. Climbed the front stairs and moved along a central hallway from door to door, shoving each open and looking inside. Storage room: cartons stacked haphazardly, a jumble of old-style exercise equipment pushed to one side. Videotapes spilled from an open carton near the window. An office: rolltop desk and oak file cabinets, but no papers or desk chair, obviously unused. Neatly made-up bedroom that might have belonged to a young woman: pale yellow walls, canopied bed, mirrored dressing table.

Gaby's room.

Inside I looked at the dust-covered things laid out on the top of the dressing table: half-full perfume vial, Chanel No. 19; manicure and pedicure kit; brush and comb; various ointments and creams; makeup from Prescriptives, a firm that had by now gone out of business.

Nothing had changed since Gaby's death.

A rocking chair was pulled up to a rear window overlooking a small yard where a marble fountain splashed. The chair, I was sure, where Clarence Drew's wife had kept her vigil after Gaby had "ruined" their lives by "getting herself killed." I wondered what thoughts had passed through the woman's mind. Sorrow and loneliness, yes, but something more. I could feel its presence in the room.

Guilt.

Why? Because Gaby had come to them and been shunted off to boarding school for much of the time? Because they had failed to love her as parents would? Because Mrs. Drew knew her husband was molesting the girl and had done nothing to stop it? Because Gaby had been murdered on their watch?

All of those reasons, maybe.

I opened the closet. Not a lot of clothing there, but Gaby would have taken most of her things to Palo Alto, and Lucy Grant had disposed of them at Drew's request. What Gaby had chosen not to take with her was telling: school uniforms, penny loafers, preppy plaid skirts, demure little blouses. Gaby had exchanged her girl's wardrobe for that of a college woman.

I went through the rest of the room, but found nothing of interest. Most of the drawers were empty except for some ruffled young-girl's nightgowns, shabby underwear, and junk jewelry. No secret hiding places, no clues to her inner life. What remained were simply discards.

Time to get out of there. I was trespassing, on dangerous ground. I started for the staircase, but an odd creaking noise from the next room attracted me. The door was half open, so I went over and looked into a bedroom full of more ponderous mahogany furnishings and—

And in its center a large man's body hanging from a rope tied around a high beam.

The chair Clarence Drew had apparently been standing on—a desk model, probably the one from the office—lay on its side beneath the dangling legs. The body sagged, dead weight, but moved slightly in a breeze from an open window. The odors of urine and feces permeated the air.

I've seen victims of violence—self-inflicted or otherwise—many times, but I've never become indifferent to them. My breath caught, and I backed away from the door, stood in the hallway breathing shallowly. An old friend who could frequently be found with her mouth and nose in a paper bag to avoid hyperventilating had taught me that too much intake of oxygen after a shock could lead to disorientation and loss of consciousness. In the absence of a bag, little breaths worked.

After a couple of minutes I went back to the door. There was no doubt that Drew was dead; his face was deeply purple and even at a distance I could tell his neck was broken.

I glanced around the room, looking for a suicide note. Found it on the bureau next to a pile of loose change.

> I HAVE NO ONE FROM WHOM TO ASK FOR FORGIVE-
> NESS. MY WILL AND OTHER DOCUMENTS ARE IN THE
> SAFE AT MY OFFICE.

Short, and not sweet.
I backed out of the room and called 911.

"So we meet again, Ms. McCone," Inspector Devlin Fast said. "But this time I know more of your history."

We were sitting at the table in the kitchen of Clarence Drew's house. Through the closed door I could hear the sounds of the paramedics removing Drew's body. They'd taken longer to arrive than the animal rescue group I'd called to take custody of Drew's frightened little dog.

"My history," I said.

"Long career, high-profile cases. The Diplo-bomber, for instance. More than your usual fifteen minutes' worth of fame, more sound bites."

"Just doing my job."

"Don't tell me you didn't enjoy the attention."

I sat up straighter. "I wasn't looking for publicity, if that's what you mean. It's not helpful in my profession. And I don't get off on people's pain and misery."

Fast looked skeptical. "And you've built up a nice business."

"I don't see where that's any problem. We've helped a lot of people over the years."

He smiled thinly. "You do stand up for yourself. I like that."

Why the sudden shift? To disarm me so I'd tell him what he wanted to know?

"Now," he said, "what were you doing here at Mr. Drew's house?"

I explained the sequence of events.

"But *why* did you come here?"

"As I told you in my previous statement about the Chuck Bosworth case, I'm writing a true-crime account of the Gabriella DeLucci murder. I needed to ask Mr. Drew some questions."

"Ah, yes, your book. Who's the publisher?"

"It's on spec." A term I had heard Rae use.

"Well, I hope you find a home for it and it sells well. These recent slayings will undoubtedly spice it up." He looked down at the plastic evidence bag containing Drew's suicide note. "What do you make of this?"

"Drew was an arrogant man. He was suspected of having molested his legal ward, Gaby DeLucci, and there's a good chance he did. But even in his last message he wouldn't admit it. In his eyes he'd done nothing wrong."

"That's a pretty insightful analysis of a man you say you've met only once."

"I've met his kind before. I've read case histories and the SFPD's file on the DeLucci murder. And I've visited FreeToHarm.com."

Fast's eyes narrowed at my mention of the site. "Oh, yes, the watchdogs."

"They're performing a service."

"And hurting a lot of innocent people along the way. Anybody with a grudge—"

"I realize that. I'm just as aware of the site's potential for harm as you are. And so was Drew; he realized that other people weren't going to take the same casual attitude toward the molestations that he did. His life and career were essentially over. There were five postings about Drew and Gaby in the last two weeks."

"Only two weeks? The DeLucci girl's been dead for two years."

"Apparently somebody's decided to stir the hornet's nest."

# Mick Savage

He was plenty pissed off by the time he got back to San Francisco. Pissed at the airline—his flight had been late leaving Portland—pissed at traffic, pissed at himself. The latter because he'd neglected to find out the identity of the friend—Marco—who had e-mailed Tullock about the NA meeting. He could e-mail him, of course, but it wouldn't be the same as speaking with him in person. Mick wondered how Shar would feel about additional air ticket charges on the old expense account if he had to fly back up there.

Nothing was happening at the pier. Late-afternoon lull. Ted and Kendra had their heads together over a spreadsheet. Patrick was conferring with Thelia Chen. Rae was absent, as were Shar and Julia. Craig Morland and Adah Joslyn, the remaining operatives, were in Italy on their honeymoon.

When Mick went into his own office, Derek was working at his keyboard and held up a hand to indicate he couldn't be disturbed.

One good thing with Shar gone, Mick thought, he wouldn't have to fess up to his laxity on the Portland end of the investigation.

Mick booted up his Mac and fired off a message to Marco's address. Then he checked his mail: nothing of importance, but he hadn't expected there to be.

At a loss for anything else to do, he began a search on Marco.

Marco Pinole, age thirty-six. Address in Amity, Oregon, not too many miles from Tullock's ranch. Listed phone number. Occupation: crop duster. Wife, thirty-four, named Serena. Two sons, William, age eight, and Anthony, age six.

No municipal airport in Amity, three private strips, permission required before landing. A crop duster would likely be located at one of them, or maybe at a grass or gravel strip that had no FAA designation.

No message yet from Marco Pinole. Mick picked up the phone and called the listed number.

"No, Marco's not here now," the youngish female voice said. "This is his wife. May I help you?"

"I'm calling about a crop-dusting job. When will he be back?"

"Not until morning; he's out on a charter."

"Sorry I missed him. I didn't know he also flies charters."

"He doesn't, all that much, but this was a favor to some friends of his."

"Friends, plural? In a little crop-dusting plane?"

She laughed. "No, we have a Cessna that can carry

four passengers—more if, like today, there're children in the party."

"D'you have any idea where he was going?"

Hesitation. "Canada, I think. Probably Vancouver. He took his passport."

"Is that usual for him? To fly charters to Canada?"

"As I said, this was a favor to a friend. Look, Mr...."

"Savage. Mick Savage." He gave her his number.

"I'll see he gets back to you." She hung up.

So the Tullocks were on their way to Canada with very little, if any, baggage. Running scared.

# Sharon McCone

I had an edge on the SFPD: while I'd been waiting for them to arrive at Clarence Drew's house I'd located an address book in a kitchen drawer that listed all the household help. The name of the maid who had fled the scene was Carlita Yanez, and she lived in Pacifica, a small city on the sea some twenty miles south of the city.

I drove down there as soon as Inspector Fast told me I could leave. Yanez's home was in the Sharp Park area, which extends from the beach inland; looming on a hill above it is a dour-looking gray stone edifice called Sam's Castle. I knew a woman who had written a book about the Bay Area's oddities, and she'd told me that the castle had been constructed in the early 1900s by a railroad baron and sold in the fifties to a man named Sam Mazza, who had more or less partied his life away there. Since his death in mid-2000 it has been in historic trust and under renovation.

To me it looked more like a place to hurl oneself off the cliff in despair than a party house.

The maid's home was on a side street directly below the castle. Modest, brown-shingled, overhung by old oaks and eucalypti, a small deck wrapping around on both sides. I went up the front steps and rang the bell. No one came to the door, but a curtain in a window to the left moved.

"Ms. Yanez," I called. "My name is Sharon McCone. I was at Clarence Drew's house when you found him today."

No answer.

"I need to talk with you before the police do. It's very important."

Silence, but I sensed she'd come over to the other side of the door.

"Please, Ms. Yanez. I'm a private investigator. I can help you deal with this."

The door opened a crack. Big, thickly lashed dark eyes stared out at me over a safety chain.

"I promised my husband I would speak to no one until he returns from his work tonight."

"As I said, it's very important that you talk to me."

"The police..."

"Will be here shortly. I'm affiliated with them," I lied.

Hesitation. Then she undid the security chain, slipped outside, and shut the door behind her. "Not inside. Out here on the deck."

She led me to a white plastic table with an umbrella and four chairs. We sat down facing each other. Her lips were trembling and she compulsively wrung her hands. Her long, polished fingernails were chipped and jagged as if she'd been biting them.

"Mr. Drew," she said, and shuddered, "it was terrible."

"Do you know of any reason he might have taken his own life?"

"I have been thinking about that. He was not the same these past weeks."

"How d'you mean?"

"He was very nervous. He didn't notice if I left something undone. He didn't eat the meals I prepared for him."

"You say 'these past weeks.' How many?"

"Two, maybe three."

"Did anything unusual happen before or during that time?"

She considered, her sad eyes narrowing. "No. But yesterday he stayed home from his office and something happened then. When I came back from an errand, he was at the top of the outside steps, shouting at a woman halfway down. It looked as if she had fallen, or maybe he'd pushed her. She was shouting too, but when she saw me she went away fast. Mr. Drew was very red in the face afterward and wouldn't talk to me."

"Did you recognize the woman?"

"No."

"Can you describe her?"

"Small, like me. But much lighter hair . . . what is called dirty blond, I think. But I was much more worried about Mr. Drew than her, so I didn't look closely." She sighed. "And today, he has done this terrible thing to himself." She crossed herself. "A cardinal sin."

A red pickup truck pulled to the curb in front, and a handsome, stocky man got out. "My husband, Tony," she said, standing.

Tony Yanez came up onto the deck, his eyes wary. His

wife introduced us, told him who I was. I showed him my license to confirm my ID.

"You all right, babe?" he asked her.

"All right—now."

He was still suspicious. He sat down next to her, put a hand on her arm, and said to me, "What's the deal? Why are you here?"

"I was at the Drew house when your wife found his body."

"So?"

"I'm assisting the police with their investigation." That explanation satisfied almost everyone; Tony was no exception. He nodded.

I said to Carlita Yanez, "Just a few more questions. How did Mr. Drew seem when you went to work today?"

"He was upstairs when I got there, and he was very short with me. He said he didn't want to be disturbed, that I should clean only downstairs."

"Was he often short with you?"

"Never, except when I asked if I should clean that room with the door that's always closed. I was not to go in there, no matter what. I think it belonged to a daughter who died."

"Did you go in?"

She colored. "Twice. It was such a pretty room, and so sad. I wanted to dust and polish the furniture, but I was afraid Mr. Drew would discover and fire me."

I pictured the scene in Drew's bedroom. "When you found him, did you notice anything else out of place or strange?"

"I didn't look. As soon as I saw him, I ran out." A pause. "But . . . yes, there *was* something. Some boxes that are usually kept in the storage room—old VHS tapes, but there's no TV in the bedroom." She paused. Then, "Earlier, in the den where the entertainment center is, I found DVDs taken from their cabinet and stacked on the floor. And in the foyer I found this. I was going to put it in the garbage, but I forgot."

From her jeans pocket she showed me a red-white-and-blue drinking straw, flattened and twisted like a tiny noose.

My skin prickled.

Darcy.

As I drove back from Pacifica, I tried to imagine what Darcy had been doing in Clarence Drew's house. Of course, Drew might have picked the straw up somewhere else.

*And how many times does a coincidence like that happen?*

Unlike many people, I believe in coincidence. I've encountered evidence of it any number of times in my investigations. But, believer that I am, this was too much of a leap. Darcy had been in that house.

Before or after Drew died? And why?

Tony Yanez had been right: this was a job for the police. If it hadn't been for that twisted straw, I'd have been glad to let them have it.

Something else nagged at me as I approached the pier; I left my car in its slot below the agency's catwalk and walked down to Red's Java House, bought fish and chips and a Coke, and sat down outside on the low concrete wall facing the Bay. The fresh, balmy salt air and good food sparked my mental processes, and I soon realized what had been bothering me.

Both Mr. George, the apartment manager in Palo Alto, and Will Smead, the faculty advisor, had implied that Lucy Bellassis and Gaby DeLucci had been best friends. Lucy herself had said so. But didn't best friends share intimate details of their lives? Wouldn't Lucy have known Drew was molesting Gaby? Have known about the crowd Gaby ran with the summer before she started at Stanford? Wouldn't Lucy have reported those things to the police when Gaby was murdered?

Well, maybe she hadn't known. There were things in my own past that I'd never told anybody, even Hy. Nothing major, and nothing I felt guilty about any more, just things the people I cared about didn't need to know. Rae and I were best friends, but we both harbored secrets.

Or maybe Lucy had known about Gaby and Drew and decided it was wise to keep the knowledge to herself.

Either way, another talk with her was the next order of business.

# Darcy Blackhawk

*Tell me everything about that time....*

He closed his eyes, hearing the shushing in his ears. Even though he was seated, he swayed slightly from the vertigo. The little brown girl moved, rippling the mattress, and that made it worse.

"Darcy? Are you okay?"

*No no no.*

He shook his head.

"Come on, it's all right to remember."

Now he wagged his head from side to side, hard.

"Darcy—"

He put his hands over his ears. Moaned.

"How long have you been in the city?"

"Don't know."

"How *long*?"

"I...can't...remember."

"Yes, you can."

A vision of Lady Laura's cold dead face flashed before him.

*What I did...*

His head was pounding and nausea welled up. He took his hands from his ears and clasped his arms around his knees, drawing them up to his chest. And then he began to cry.

"How long?"

"I don't remember."

She glared at him. Where had that sweet, understanding smile gone?

"I can't," he repeated.

"Look, you asshole, Clarence Drew is dead! I heard it on the news. We can't get into that house again, not ever. So you better tell me—where are those tapes?"

Acid fluid was rising into his mouth. He tried to make it to the edge of the bed, but there wasn't enough time. He puked on the spread.

The girl kicked him with her high-heeled boot, knocked him off the bed. He lay stunned on the floor. Then she wasn't there any more. Gone. All gone.

*Tell me everything about that time....*

# Sharon McCone

The Bellassises had a pool—a rarity in the city. It was glassed in, with a retractable canopy, and was surrounded by lounge furniture and citrus trees planted in big pots. This evening, with the onset of dusk and fog lurking on the horizon, floodlights were on and tall gas heaters burning. Lucy led me out there and lay down on one of the chairs, a margarita glass and half-full pitcher on the table next to her.

She waved lazily to me. "Have a seat," she said, motioning at the lounge on the other side of the table. "Have a drink, there's an extra glass over on the wet bar."

I took the chair, declined the drink. Lucy wore a black bikini under a white lace cover-up; her face was a smooth, untroubled mask. "So what's happening?" she asked.

"I came here to talk with you about Clarence Drew and Gaby. It's even more urgent now: Drew is dead. He committed suicide this afternoon."

Lucy sat up straighter. "He *what*?"

I explained the circumstances.

"God," Lucy said after a long silence. "I'm not going to pretend to be sorry. If I'd had my way somebody would've killed the bastard years ago."

"You knew he was molesting Gaby, then."

"...I knew. She told me when we were freshmen in high school, swore me to secrecy. There seemed to be some sort of...complicity between her and Drew. Or maybe she was afraid of hurting his wife. Or maybe it had just been going on so long."

"Did Park also know?"

"Not then, but I finally told him."

"When?"

"A few weeks ago, August nineteenth—it would've been Gaby's twentieth birthday. For the first time I got it together and put flowers on her grave. But seeing that crappy cemetery and the weeds on the grave got me all worked up. I came home and had too much to drink and ranted to Park about Drew and what he'd done to Gaby."

"What was Park's reaction?"

"He was shocked, of course. And upset. He made me tell him everything I knew about it, which isn't much; Gaby was pretty reticent. Park said we ought to have Drew arrested, but how could we? With Gaby dead, there's no proof. The next morning he said he'd thought it over and decided it was ancient history. We should just let things be. Ancient history! Only two years ago!"

"Why do you think Park backed off?"

Lucy slugged some of her margarita before she answered. "Drew still has a lot of power and influence in the state and federal governments. I guess Park was afraid for his career, and I don't blame him. The FAA has been looking closely at his company for some reason. Any hint of a scandal, you know..."

"Did he tell you that?"

"Not in so many words. But what other reason would he have for covering up for Clarence?"

Yes, what other reason?

# Mick Savage

Clarence Drew was my last lead to Darcy," Shar said on the phone, "and now he's dead."

She sounded tired. Well, no wonder: she was working her butt off to find her asshole half brother.

Mick stared out at the string of lights on the Embarcadero, clearly visible from Alison's condo on the twenty-fifth floor of the Millennium Tower, a luxury high-rise south of Market. She'd bought it with an inheritance from her grandmother and now realized the lifestyle was not for her, but she was stuck with it until real estate prices rebounded.

He asked Shar, "Are you at the agency?"

"Yes."

"Maybe you should ease up some."

"I know I should—and I will. Hy's coming back from Switzerland late tonight, and I want to spend time with him. Of course, he'll probably sleep for twenty-four hours."

"You could do with twenty-four hours yourself."

"Mick." Her tone was sharp. "I know what I could do with. I don't need to be told." Then, mellowing, "Sorry. This has all been very upsetting. I'm only doing it for Saskia's sake, you know."

"Maybe it would be better for everybody if Darcy disappeared for good."

"I don't think so. The not knowing—"

"Is worse than knowing for sure."

"Right."

Alison appeared with two glasses of a good Zin they'd found on their last visit to the Alexander Valley, then took her own and retreated to the den. Her one weakness was a soap opera, *All My Children*, which she DVR'd for viewing when she had the time. Mick liked the soap okay, not that he watched it much, but he wondered why all its seemingly otherwise intelligent characters wanted to live in Pine Valley, Pennsylvania, where all sorts of horrible things kept happening to them.

He asked Shar, "Are you still determined to trace Tick Tack Jack?"

"Yes."

"Vancouver, BC, is a big city. Not much hope of locating Tullock and his family."

"I'm not so sure of that. There's an agency I know of up there—Phyllis Brent and Associates. We could use them."

"How high are you willing to go on the cost?"

"They'll trade for favors."

"Meaning lost profits for us."

"I'll absorb them. I can afford it, don't worry."

"Who? Me? I'm just your dumbass nephew."

"Yeah. And you don't worry—just like I don't worry about you."

Alison had an early meeting in the morning, so Mick opted to sleep at his condo. Once there, though, he felt at loose ends. Nothing he liked on TV, as usual. He got onto YouTube and checked out a few postings of crime-scene reenactments about stupid criminals. There was the burglar who hid from the police under a bunch of plastic garbage bags—with the money and jewelry he'd taken still in his pockets. The bank robber who thought the FBI would have to give him back the loot after he got out of prison—"Hey, I *earned* it!" The kidnapper who wrote a ransom note on the back of one of his checking account deposit slips. God, they made the human race look as if it were composed of idiots!

And that made him think of Darcy.

Shar's demented half brother was creeping around the area leaving a trail of twisted red-white-and-blue straws to rival Hansel and Gretel's breadcrumbs. He wasn't what you'd call a linear thinker, but there had to be some explanation for his behavior. Mick tried to put himself in Darcy's shoes by remembering the times when he'd been really drunk or stoned. None of them, not even when he'd taken LSD and seen cat hair growing out of the water in the kitchen sink, enlightened him as to what must be going on in Darcy's mind. Drunk, drugged, or sober, Mick had always had a sense of himself and his where-abouts. That, he suspected, was not so with old Darce.

On impulse he began a series of searches on Darcy's background. Arrested for kiting checks, shoplifting, possession of various illegal substances, loitering, and jaywalking. Caught stealing beer steins from a German restaurant. Walked out in a two-hundred-dollar pair of shoes he'd been trying on at Macy's. Driven off to avoid paying at a gas station, with the hose still connected to his pickup, then wrecked said pickup and two other cars, narrowly avoiding DUIs. Yet he'd done minimal jail time.

Mick sensed the hand of Saskia Blackhawk protecting her baby boy.

Why, for God's sake?

Well, she was his mother. No one knew why mothers did the things that they did. Although Mick suspected what *his* mother would've done in the same situation: she'd've let him sit in jail and then yelled at him every chance she had for a whole year after he got out. After he'd been caught hacking into the Pacific Palisades Board of Education's records, she and his father had banished him to San Francisco to work for Shar. Indentured servitude, he'd thought at the time. Best thing that had ever happened to him, he thought now.

Back to Darcy: he was indeed stupid. All of this was petty crime. The jerk didn't have it in him to pull off anything clever.

Enough, he told himself. Enough. A drink, something mind-numbing on TV, and sleep.

# SATURDAY, SEPTEMBER 11

# Sharon McCone

September 11.

Nine-eleven.

The day the hijacked planes crashed into the Pentagon and a field in Pennsylvania and brought down New York City's Twin Towers. The day we knew that, as a nation, we'd never be completely safe again.

Safety has a lot of meanings. Personal safety: lock your doors; arm your alarm systems; look both ways when crossing the street. Have annual doctor's checkups; take your vitamins; don't turn your back on the ocean; cliffs crumble.

But the safety of a nation? How can you control that? There is no way to guard against hijacked planes, hurricanes, massive oil spills, earthquakes. But far worse is the steady rot from within, as society splinters and fragments and no side gives ground on any important issue.

Thinly masked racial hatred, each religion claiming that its dogma is the only way to salvation, apathy, the closing of formerly open minds. Fear is a rotten emotion, and in one way or another it had us all in its grip.

In my dreams this morning I was flying. But over desolate terrain with no sign of human habitation. Heaps of rubble that once had been cities; ravaged farmland; rivers running red; seas shrinking to puddles. No place to land, no reason to either, and in a short time I'd be out of fuel. Then I'd go out in a sputter of the engine and a swift, spiraling descent—

"McCone?" Hy said. "You all right?" His hand was warm on my shoulder.

"Unnh?"

"You were moaning and twitching."

I flopped onto my back, wiped my sweaty face with my forearm. Hy's blondish-gray curly hair was tousled, his swooping mustache feathered out on one side so his rough-hewn face looked unbalanced. And his eyes— brown, flecked with gold—were concerned.

"I was dreaming," I said. "The date..."

"Yeah." He gripped my shoulder harder. I hadn't lost anyone in the terrorist attack, but he had: RI's New York offices had been located on the seventy-second floor of the North Tower; all 102 employees had died.

We were silent for a long time, remembering the ways in which our world had changed forever.

Then he said, "So what's happening with Darcy?" We'd had more important things to do than talk when he'd arrived after two this morning.

I explained as best I could. "I'm beginning to have a bad feeling about this. He most certainly needed money;

he didn't bother Robin or Saskia because Robin's made it clear she's had it with him and Saskia would have insisted he get help, possibly have him institutionalized. He probably thought he could hit me up for some, but he hasn't been in touch since last Tuesday."

"Maybe he got it from somebody else."

"He doesn't know people with money to spare."

"From some kind of job?"

I just gave him a look.

"Knocked over a liquor store?"

"Not smart enough. This is a guy who tried to shoplift a whole ham by stuffing it under his hoodie, remember?"

"Maybe somebody's taking care of him, then. He's kind of scabrous, but there are people who enjoy the challenge of rehabbing losers."

"A woman," I said.

I sat up and began ticking off items on my fingers. "We know he was with a woman at the Palace of the Legion of Honor. We have a description of her that sounds as if she's a retro hippie. She probably took him to the cemetery in Colma where Gaby DeLucci's buried. She may even have been with him when he came here in the middle of the night. Mick did what he could to identify her, but there just wasn't enough to go on. He gave up and reassigned it to Derek, who's had no results either."

"Could she be the same woman who visited Clarence Drew the day before he hanged himself? The one the maid thought he'd thrown out?"

"No way of knowing."

"Okay," Hy said. "Drew had been having sex with Gaby—maybe he was also one of those guys who likes to watch."

"Wouldn't surprise me. But why would he want to leave evidence lying around?"

"Maybe he thought his home was impregnable."

"What, that puny dog I found hiding in the cupboard was going to ward off intruders?"

"Did he have a security system?"

"Inspector Fast said it wasn't functioning."

"Disabled?"

"Frayed wire in the outside box. It's an old system, so it could've just given out."

"Or been helped out."

"...Right."

"D'you think Darcy has any knowledge of alarm systems?"

"I doubt it."

"Someone else tampered with it, then."

"Who?"

He shrugged. "You'll find out."

Yes, but how? And where to start? If experts like Mick and Derek couldn't identify the woman who had been with Darcy, I certainly didn't stand a chance. And if the SFPD hadn't a clue as to who had tampered with Drew's security system—if, in fact, it had been tampered with—I couldn't come up with one either.

In the shower I reviewed my mental list of people connected with the case. It was pitifully short: the Nobody and Lady Laura were dead, as was Clarence Drew; Tick Tack Jack and his family had disappeared into Canada. Everybody else I'd talked with was peripheral, except for Lucy and Park Bellassis, and I sensed I'd wrung all the information from them that I was going to get.

Hy was off to RI headquarters—his way of keeping busy on this most painful of days. The neighborhood was Saturday quiet. Quieter, maybe, than usual.

I puttered around the house with Alex and Jessie underfoot, pointedly avoiding the newspaper and its rehashes of 9/11. Finally I called Mick, who sounded despondent.

"Alison's off at one of the commemorative services," he said. "She wanted me to go, but I'd rather do my remembering in private."

"I get you. How about putting in some overtime?"

"Sure—work's supposed to be good for what ails you."

"Okay, here's the deal...."

# Mick Savage

He left his bike in the driveway of Rae's and his father's sprawling house on the bluff above China Beach and went around to the kitchen door, where he saw Rae and Mrs. Wellcome having coffee in the breakfast nook. They waved for him to join them and, after pouring himself a mug from the space-age machine on the counter, he squeezed in beside Rae.

"Shar's assigned me to your neighbors," he said.

"The Bellassises, you mean."

"Right."

"She really think they're involved in these deaths?"

"I don't know. What can you tell me about them?"

Rae glanced at Mrs. Wellcome, who said, "The marriage is troubled. The husband is absent a lot, and the wife seldom leaves the house. She drinks."

"Anything else?"

"A car comes and goes. A red Honda. It pulls into the garage, and you can't see the people in it."

"How often does it come?"

"A few times a week."

"How long does it stay?"

"Half an hour, no more than an hour."

Rae said, "It could belong to Lucy's sister, Torrey Grant. Or Torrey's boyfriend, Jeff Morgan. Apparently they come over a lot to borrow stuff or use Park's computer. Lucy doesn't get along with them, but she allows it."

"Why, I wonder?" he said.

"You know how families are."

*Oh yes, I was an expert in that area.*

Mrs. Wellcome said, "My kitchen window over the sink allows me a view of the Bellassis garage. I make a point of knowing what goes on in this neighborhood."

Rae said, "Mrs. Wellcome is an honorary operative of the agency. And extremely perceptive."

The housekeeper gave her employer a look that said, "Don't patronize me, you twit."

Mick grinned widely. He said, "So it's pretty hard to keep track of what goes on over there at the Bellassis house?"

"At any house. This is hardly a neighborhood where you can peer over the back fence or into windows."

"And I suppose if I kept a surveillance, I'd stand out."

"On that motorcycle of yours?" Mrs. Wellcome snorted. "Someone would call the police and tell them the Hell's Angels were taking over."

"What about on foot?"

"Nobody walks here. Unless they have a dog. And we don't have one on hand right now."

"Sometimes kids walk," Rae said, "but there aren't a lot of them around here."

Mick eyed her thoughtfully. "Didn't you say Molly and Lisa are here this weekend?" His younger sisters lived with his mother and stepfather in Bel Air, but they spent every other weekend with Ricky and Rae.

"Yes, and they've been moping around all morning because Ricky and his band are rehearsing downstairs in the studio. I banished them to the Hellhole."

She sounded irritated. Mick knew Rae had never considered herself cut out for parenthood; still, she enjoyed the girls' visits and gave in easily—too easily—to their numerous demands.

Mrs. Wellcome said, "Better the girls be in my kitchen than that band." Soon the practice session would be over, and the kitchen would be crowded with five hungry men foraging for sandwich makings and guzzling beer. "They have no respect for order."

"Why don't you ask Lisa and Molly up here?" Mick said.

"Why, when we have this little moment of peace?"

"I need to deputize them."


"You mean like in a posse?" Lisa, the chubby blonde, was a fan of *Gunsmoke* reruns.

"Sort of," Mick said. "No horses, though. All you have to do is play whatever it is you play on the sidewalk and keep watch on a certain house."

Molly, dark and slender, frowned. "I don't think we've ever played on a sidewalk."

"Not even hopscotch?"

"What's hopscotch?"

Ah, the overprivileged life. "Well, do you know how to play cards?"

"Go fish," Lisa said. "I always win."

"How about playing go fish on the sidewalk while you watch this house for me?"

"Is that allowed?" Lisa was very concerned with rules. Nobody could imagine where she'd gotten that trait from.

"Yes, it's allowed."

Molly said, "I was gonna watch a video."

"The video will be here when you're done."

"It sounds like work. *Lots* of work. We ought to be compensated."

"Compensated." Out of young mouths big, greedy words come.

Mick sighed. "Five bucks apiece."

They looked at each other and rolled their eyes. Small change.

"Five bucks apiece," Rae said, "or I'll tell your father you both peed in your Aunt Shar's cat box during your last visit."

"We didn't!"

"Anyway," Lisa said, "it's Alex and Jessie's cat box."

"Same thing. Do you and Mick have an agreement?"

In unison, "...I guess."

"Good," Mick said. "Here's what I want you to do."

# Sharon McCone

Phyllis Brent called me from Vancouver, BC, at four-thirty that afternoon.

"We've located Jack Tullock and his family," she said. "They're staying with friends, Harrison and Lily Jackson, outside of Kelowna."

"Where's that?"

"Northwest of here, in the center of the province. Beautiful town on Okanagan Lake. Do you want us to continue surveillance?"

"Until you hear otherwise from me. What's the nearest airport?"

"Kelowna International." Phyllis laughed wryly. "Don't ask about the 'International.' Horizon Air flies to SeaTac, where you can catch a feeder flight."

"How long a trip to Kelowna?"

"From San Francisco? Over fifteen hours, with two plane changes and layovers."

God, the thought of half a day on one of those turbo-props that Horizon operates put a chill on me. I merely said, "I'll let you know my ETA."

I set down the phone, thought for a moment, then called Hy. "Where are the RI jets currently?" I asked. The company had a fleet of three, but their exact location was hard for an outsider to keep track of.

"One's in Mexico City, another in Chicago. The Citation's here."

"I need a ride to Kelowna, BC. Will you take me?"

"When?"

"Soonest."

"I'll start preflighting." Hy loved flying RI's Cessna Citation, an eight-seat jet and the fastest civilian plane in existence. I wasn't qualified to pilot it, but I'd taken the controls a number of times when we were up together, and it made Two-Seven-Tango, our Cessna 170B, seem like a slug.

It was six in the evening and the sun was well above the horizon when we took off, but soon it sank, a brilliant red sphere on the horizon. It made me think of our platform overlooking Bootleggers' Cove on the Mendocino Coast, where we'd shared so many sunsets. We hadn't been to Touchstone in a while, or to the ranch that Hy had inherited from his stepfather near Tufa Lake in the high desert, and I missed them both.

The thought of owning three paid-off properties would have thrilled most people, but since I loved them all it made me feel divided. When I was walking the cliff at Touchstone I'd long for King, my horse in the high country. At the ranch I'd ride King, wishing we were on a bluff trail above the sea. And at home in the city everyday life would sometimes consume me.

Well, it was a classy predicament.

Hy said, "The rental-car situation at Kelowna is good; I booked us a midsize with Enterprise. And customs is reported to be fairly easy. You did remember your passport?"

"I'm not a child." I realized I sounded short with him. "Sorry. This case is really getting to me. Saskia called before I left the pier, all bent out of shape. Darcy's given her so much trouble that I'm not sure he's worth finding."

"Maybe whatever's going on will have knocked some sense into him."

"Nobody's ever used the word 'sense' in connection with Darcy."

We fell silent as the western sky flamed red, purple, and gold.

# Mick Savage

Lisa came running into the kitchen at a little past six, as Mick and Rae and Ricky were talking of having the leftovers from the band's foraging for dinner. The musicians, most of whom lived in the LA area, had left to fly home or visit friends and lovers in the city.

"The red car's backing out of the garage," Lisa announced. "Molly's maintaining surveillance."

*Too many cop shows on TV.*

"Thanks, honey." Mick wiped his hands on a dish towel. "Wish me luck," he said to Rae and Ricky.

He'd left his bike parked nose-out in the driveway. The engine thrummed and he eased out onto the street where the red Honda was just turning the corner toward the avenues. Molly, on the sidewalk, saluted him as he drove past.

\*　　\*　　\*

He lost the red Honda in the clog of Saturday evening traffic on Geary, spotted it again as it turned onto Masonic. As near as he could tell there was only one occupant, the driver. From the shape of the head and the haircut, it looked to be a man. So it couldn't be Lucy's sister, Torrey Grant, but perhaps her boyfriend, Jeff Morgan.

Across the leafy Panhandle of Golden Gate Park and uphill to Clayton Street. A swift left into another driveway and garage. Gone.

The house looked to be an apartment building—one long flat on each story, and perhaps a smaller unit behind the garage. A Victorian, Italianate, with thick balustrades, cornices under the eaves, and steep steps slanting across the façade to a small front porch. Somewhat shabby, beige paint cracked and flaking. A typical rental with an absentee landlord and an agent or tenants who didn't give a damn, he thought.

It was after nine o'clock and mostly dark. Lights shone between curtained windows, and a TV flickered on the second floor. Mick was hungry and thirsty and unhappy with himself because he'd violated one of Shar's unbreakable rules: always carry bottled water and an energizing snack in your car because you never know when you might have to run a surveillance.

Would he ever learn? Probably not. But then it wouldn't matter, if he kept his promise to himself not to do any more fieldwork.

Occasionally shadows crossed the window coverings, but none were identifiable. He wondered what the hell he was doing here. But something about that car and the way it had been driven bothered him. Something erratic and furtive.

He waited.

\*   \*   \*

It was eleven when he ran out of patience. He'd studied the house and realized there was no way around it from the street to its rear, so he'd devised a cover story to gain access.

He crossed the street, went up the old marble steps, and studied the mailboxes. Four. So there was an apartment in the basement. Labels from top to bottom: Bartlett; Carver; a blank and another blank. He rang the last bell anyway, thinking that a person wouldn't be likely to come all the way up to the foyer, but might buzz him in.

There was no reply. Okay, there were lights on the second and third floors. He buzzed the second.

A man answered. Mick said, "Fire inspector. I need to check the wiring."

"On a Saturday night? Christ! I suppose you're being paid overtime for this."

"There's been a complaint—"

"Yeah, well, I got a complaint too. You people are raking it in and it's all coming out of my taxes."

"Sir, we have a report of a potentially dangerous situation on the top floor."

"Only dangerous situation up there don't have nothing to do with wiring."

"And what does that mean?"

"Ah, fuck it." The door buzzer went off and the intercom went silent.

Mick stepped into the foyer. Musty, none-too-clean-old-building smell; narrow stairs slanting upward toward a landing. At one time this would have been a fine old residence, but now the carpets were worn, the wallpaper peeling, and most of the lightbulbs burned out.

He rapped on the door of the first-floor unit. As he'd expected from the lack of lights, there was no response.

Okay, farthest place next.

After his knock at the top-floor unit, he heard murmurs, footsteps, a female voice saying, "Yes?"

"Fire inspector."

The door opened and a woman with her hair in curlers looked out. Pink plastic curlers, the likes of which Mick hadn't seen since he was a child.

From the interior of the apartment a rough male voice said, "Angie, get your ass back in here before I come out there and tear you a new one."

"It's some fire inspector."

"I don't care if it's Jesus Christ himself. Shut the door and get back here."

"Fuck off!"

"You telling me to fuck off? I'll show you—"

The woman slammed the door.

Right: the potentially dangerous situation here had to do not with the wiring of the building but with the faulty wiring of two people.

Mick descended the staircase, paused at the second-floor apartment. Except for the fact that he was Caucasian, the man who had buzzed him in resembled a sumo wrestler.

"You don't look like no fire inspector," he said.

"They called me in unexpectedly. I didn't have time to put on my uniform. Do you know the other tenants here?"

The man glowered at him, seemed about to shut the door without answering, and then changed his mind. "What the hell," he said. "There's the Battlin' Bartletts"— his thumb jerked at the ceiling—"and the couple on first.

Don't know their names, but they're young, just slumming. Right now they're in Carmel and a year from now they'll be living in Cow Hollow."

"Can you describe them?"

"She's kind of little, but strong. Works out a lot. I think her hair's blond, but I'm not sure. His is. He's big, built. Guess he works out too."

"Do you know what they do for a living?"

The man shook his head. "She's in and out all the time, might not work. He's gone overnight a lot, some kind of salesman, maybe. Say, how come a fire inspector's askin' these kinda questions?"

"I think I may know them through friends." Quickly Mick changed the subject. "I noticed four mailboxes."

"Yeah, there's a basement studio, looks out into a light well. People come and go. I think they're dealin' drugs."

"The current tenants?"

"Ain't no current tenants. The management company hasn't bothered to fill the vacancy since the people who were renting it moved out a couple of months ago."

"You know their names?"

A shrug, muscles in the big shoulders rippling. "Hilda and... something. Maybe Mack. Don't know a last name or where they went."

"And the management company?"

"Real Good Properties, over on Masonic. Stupid name."

"So these people who come and go are now squatters?"

"Not really. They just use it as a drop for drugs."

"What kind of people are they?"

"All kinds. Junk don't discriminate about the class of folks it hooks."

"Can you describe any of them?"

Another shrug. "Guys in suits, straight from the Financial district. Guys in rags, who can hardly stop shaking. Beautiful women. Ugly women. People with no teeth, people with rashes and needle tracks and infected scars. Young kids—thirteen, fourteen—bent on ruinin' their lives. Pregnant women with no regard for the babies they're carryin'. Like I said, junk don't discriminate."

A hollow feeling started under Mick's breastbone. He thought of Molly, Lisa, and his other siblings, felt grateful that they were insulated from such lives, not only by money but by love.

"Isn't there anybody you can describe in detail?" he asked.

The man shook his head. "Pretty soon they all look alike. You know what I mean?"

# Sharon McCone

After we passed through Canadian customs at Kelowna, I phoned Phyllis Brent. Her operatives had reported that no one had left the Jackson house all day, she said, and gave me directions to it. "My people will maintain surveillance in case there's any trouble."

When I ended the call I said to Hy, "She's got two operatives out there. The tab on this is going to be horrific."

"Let Saskia pay for it. She's the one who wants Darcy back. Besides, you could always write that true-crime book you've been using as an excuse for asking questions. I bet Rae's publisher would take it on."

"Great. Add to my notorious reputation. To say nothing of destroying Saskia's and Robin's privacy."

"Face it, McCone, all of this is going to come out publicly. Better you should benefit from it than somebody else. Because you know writers are going to pounce on it. Look what happened with the Diplo-bomber and the Ever-Running Man."

Yes, a couple of true-crime writers had gotten prosperous, if not rich, on those stories. The first one I'd cooperated with, only to be misquoted. I refused to speak with the second one.

"But...write? Me?"

"You just put one word after the other."

"That's simplistic. Writing isn't easy."

"Then get Rae to coauthor it."

We'd reached the rental-car counter. "We'll see," I said.


The Jackson house was on the lakeshore. By the time we reached it darkness had fallen. It was huge, of stone and wood, with large lighted windows that showed a spare contemporary interior.

I studied it, said to Hy, "At night you can just look into their lives."

"It's pretty far from any neighbors. And maybe they don't mind being looked at."

"It would make me edgy as hell."

"That's because you know what dangers the darkness holds."

As he spoke I saw two men and a woman walk into a front room carrying wineglasses. After a moment another woman joined them.

"Cozy," I said. "You wouldn't think they had a care in the world."

"The Jacksons probably don't. And the Tullocks have an illusion of safety here."

"Which I'm about to shatter."

*     *     *

Jack Tullock came warily to the door after a man—
presumably his host—called him. Tullock looked trapped
when I showed him my credentials. His eyes searched the
shadows, settling on Hy, who stood slightly behind me.

He said to his host, "Harrison, it's okay. Go back to the
party." To Hy he added, "And who the hell are you?"

"An associate of Ms. McCone." He handed him his card.

Tullock examined it, then crumpled it in the palm of
his hand. He said, "Don't you people ever stop? First that
Savage guy, now you. I got a right to my privacy."

"Not where an open murder case is concerned."

"Christ! I'm tired of hearing about it! I just want to be
left alone to live my life in peace."

"I'm sure that was what Gaby DeLucci wanted too."

"Gaby, Gaby, Gaby! I'm sick of hearing about her. Like
she was some sort of martyred saint. Well, she wasn't—
not by far."

"Why don't you tell me about her, Mr. Tullock? You
told Mr. Savage you had something to get off your chest."

"That was before—"

"Before what?"

"Before I knew my family was in danger."

"From . . . ?"

"Chuck Bosworth called, left a message that I should
watch my back. I called back twice to some bar in San
Francisco, but he was never there."

"His call made you run up here to Canada?"

"No, I had another call."

"From?"

"A woman who wouldn't identify herself. Wanted a
hundred thousand bucks to keep quiet about my past. A

hundred thou, for Chrissakes! I've got zip in the bank, and my ranch alone wouldn't bring that much."

"And that was a serious enough threat to make you abandon your home?"

"Hell yes. The woman was serious, and she knew the whole story. Knew things even I didn't."

"Why don't you tell us about those things?"

"Because they're none of your goddamn business!"

"I can make it the Yamhill County Sheriff's Department's business."

"What you're talking about happened two years ago, in another state."

"Open murder case," I said again.

"Damn you!" Pause. "I better talk to my wife." He shut the door.

Hy and I waited in the star-shot darkness. He put his hand on my shoulder and squeezed it encouragingly. After a few minutes Tullock opened the door and motioned us in. He seemed somewhat chastened after the conference with his wife.

"Beth says it's time for the truth to come out."

We followed him inside.

"Not in there," he said, motioning toward the room where the other people were gathered. "Beth's waiting for us on the patio." He led us through the house to a deck where embers glowed in a large grill and heat lamps radiated warmth. A woman sat there, hugging her arms across her breasts: a short, plump blonde whose prettiness was beginning to fade.

"This is Beth," Tullock said.

We greeted her and sat side by side on a wicker sofa.

Tullock took a chair next to Beth's and reached for her hand. "Beth knows I was pretty wild years back. Got into drugs, dumped my first wife and daughter, took off on the road. Ended up in rehab in San Francisco. Made friends with a couple of other former addicts, Laura Mercer and Chuck Bosworth. What she don't know about is the thing with Gaby DeLucci."

He looked at his wife, and she nodded encouragingly.

"Gaby was a volunteer at this place where we hung out, trying to stay straight. She pulled us all together, named us the Four Musketeers. But it turned out Gaby had an agenda: she was an orphan and her legal guardian, this prick called Clarence Drew, had been molesting her for years. Made tapes of them together, and she wanted us to steal them from his house. Not only that, she wanted him dead. Told us to take some other stuff, so it'd look like a robbery gone bad. Said she'd pay us big bucks.

"Molestation, that's pretty bad, but it ain't in me to kill somebody. Laura and Chuck, they were all for it. Gaby said she'd 'keep Drew occupied' while we got into the house. But I...What happened was all my fault. I went to see Drew, told him to leave Gaby alone and give me the tapes. He said there weren't any, it was consensual sex, and if I didn't lay off he'd call the cops."

Tullock paused, shaking his head. "With my record, what could I do?"

I said, "Did you warn Gaby about what you'd done?"

"I did. She just laughed, said Clarence wouldn't do anything. She had a 'date' with him that night, and nine o'clock was when we should break in. I was supposed to tell Laura and Chuck, but I didn't. Instead I went to a bar, made sure I was seen there, and got myself blind drunk. Next morning the headlines were all about Gaby being found dead in the park."

"Why didn't you go to the police?"

"A guy like me, going up against the likes of Clarence Drew?"

"Not even for Gaby's sake?"

"No, not for nobody's sake. Soon as I heard Gaby was dead, I split. Came up to Oregon, reconciled with my daughter. Went to work for my uncle, met Beth, and when my uncle died he left me this ranch." His smile in the glow from the coals was sardonic. "Also left me his animals. I don't understand why the hell he wanted them—especially that damned camel—but they're living creatures and I treat them the same as he did. Same way I've always treated everybody."

His eyes defied me to say, "Even Gaby?"

# Darcy Blackhawk

*I hurt all over....*

His ribs. His head. Both shoulders. His ankle.

He was lying on the floor in a small, cramped space, his face in a drying pool that smelled like puke. The little brown girl was gone. How long since she'd left him here?

If she never came back he'd die here, alone.

*No!*

Shar. She'd almost died when she was shot that time. What did they call people like her? Survivors?

If she could survive, so could he. Shared blood had to count for something.

He tried to move, but the pain was so bad it made his eyes water. Or maybe thinking of Shar had made him cry. She didn't know he was here, wherever he was, and hurting. Nobody did.

Everybody he'd ever known had forgotten him. Mom,

Robbie, Shar. Dad and Laura too, because death meant permanently forgetting. He'd never had many friends; once people got close enough to really know him, they pulled away. Okay, so maybe he wasn't like other people, but he still had feelings. He still needed to be loved.

*All alone.*

He ran his dry tongue over his lips. Tasted blood. That girl, she'd slapped him. Yanked on his hair. Kicked him in the head. Then she'd shot him full of junk.

Why?

Something she thought Lady Laura gave him. But he'd never had anything of Laura's.

Laura was dead, and the cops thought he'd done it. That was what the girl had said.

But why should he believe her, after what she'd done to him? He didn't know what to believe, what was the truth and what wasn't.

*Truth.* Mom's favorite word. Always tell the truth, truth will set you free.

*Mom. Where were you when all this weird shit happened to me? Busy. In your office. In court. Saving the Indians. Never mind about saving* this *Indian, your son.*

Things were getting fuzzy again. He forced his eyes open. Two of everything. Two bed stand rollers, two edges of a quilt, two right arms...two puncture wounds in each of those arms...

*I hurt all over....*

# Mick Savage

He was already inside the old house, and he doubted any of the people he'd talked with would prevent him from exploring. He found a door off the downstairs hallway, a padlocked one that from what he knew of the layouts of these Victorians would lead to the garage and the basement apartment. He went back there and eyed the lock. Not completely closed, as if someone wanted to make it appear secure but didn't want to trouble with the key. Mick removed the lock from the hasp and started down.

Narrow wooden stairs that ended abruptly. He misjudged the distance from the concrete floor and almost lost his balance. In his flashlight's beam he saw that the red Honda was parked in the garage. He went over to it, intending to check its registration, but the doors were all locked. He noted the plate number; he'd run it soon, but not before he searched the entire building.

A short hallway led to a door at the rear, and he went down it. That door wasn't locked either. He knocked and turned the knob, calling out. No response.

Mick stepped inside, closed the door, and fumbled for a light switch; a bare dim bulb came on overhead. He was in a small room whose only window was high up toward the ceiling, probably overlooking a light well; dark burlap curtained it. The only furnishing was a bed, its covers badly rumpled and smelling of vomit. The room reeked and was hot and stuffy; there was no sign of whoever might have occupied it. He examined the sheets and thin blanket on the bed. On the pillow there were some hairs: yellow-green.

*Darcy.*

He'd been here. Why?

Mick took a closer inventory of the basement room. A door opened off it into a tiny bathroom; it was so filthy that he hesitated before entering. A used syringe lay on the edge of the sink; he placed it in a plastic bag he found and stuffed it into an inside pocket of his jacket. Outside there were more vomit and stains that could be blood on the threadbare tan carpet. Two more yellow-green hairs and a streak of blood leading to the door.

He knelt and looked more closely at the streaks. Within them he could see individual droplets, as if Darcy had been bleeding and then had dragged his body over the stains. The blood was potentially a good sign: dead people didn't bleed. Mick stepped through the door, trained his light on the concrete floor. More droplets, many of them not smeared.

He felt the bloodstains with his fingertips. Still tacky. It hadn't been very long since Darcy had left, on his own or with help—

A rumbling noise. At first he couldn't place it. Then, on the other side of the wall, a car started up. By the time he got down the hall and into the garage the automatic door was closing.

Mick ran up the steps and out the front door. No sign of the Honda. Back inside he eyed the closed door to the first-floor apartment, then went over and tried the knob. Unlocked. God, some people were stupid!

They'd left the heat on too; it was hot in there. Mick switched on his flash and moved through the rooms, taking in the décor—lots of splashy, trashy modern art and low-slung furnishings—and looking for signs that Darcy had been there. There were none. On the coffee table he found copies of *Flying* and *Allure*. Otherwise nothing.

Okay, legitimate people on a getaway weekend. Carmel, the man upstairs had said, and next year they'd be somewhere like the exclusive Cow Hollow district. They were slumming, he'd said. It was a pattern Mick had noticed: young couples moving to the city for a taste of "real urban life" and, when that life got too real, moving to a more upscale area. One day—probably when they were expecting their first child—they'd be bound for the suburbs, a house with a yard, and a better school system. The trashy art would be left behind. It was doubtful such people even knew what had been going on in the basement of their own building.

Still he kept searching. Exactly what for he didn't know. The clothing in the closet was typical of urbanites: casual business dress, athletic attire, a dark man's suit, and a woman's cocktail dress. The bathroom cabinet contained no medicines or other indications of poor health.

Two pairs of running shoes had been kicked off in the living room.

On an end table sat a framed photograph of a couple: tanned, blond-haired, standing on a cliff with the ocean in the background. He took out his cell and snapped a picture of it.

Who were these people? And how the hell could they have any connection to Darcy?

# Sharon McCone

My cell phone interrupted the conversation with Jack Tullock. Mick. I excused myself, went to stand at the far end of the patio.

What Mick related to me left me stunned. Darcy holed up in a tiny basement apartment. Blood and vomit. Used syringes. And now, gone again.

For the first time since all this began, I felt deeply for my half brother. The fear and confusion. The helplessness. I'd never hidden—if that was indeed what he'd been doing—but I'd been imprisoned, and I knew all those emotions.

"Are you sure he's not someplace else in the building?" I asked.

"I talked with the tenants on two and three; nobody's seen him, and it's not likely any of them would be hiding him. The first-floor people are away for the weekend. They left their door unlocked."

"Mick, you didn't trespass—"

I hadn't expected him to answer that, and he didn't. "They have a framed photo, probably of themselves. I took pictures of it with my phone. I'll put them on the computer and enlarge them."

"Send them to me. You say the red Honda was there?"

"Yeah, but not any more. I'll run the plates and let you know who it's registered to. Beyond that I don't know what else I can do."

"Keep up the surveillance."

Hy and the Tullocks looked questioningly at me when I rejoined them and sat down. "Bad news?" Jack asked.

I didn't reply; my mind was still on Darcy. Had he been kidnapped? Then why no ransom demand? And why Darcy? Saskia had money, but by no means was she wealthy. Something else they wanted? What?

I feared for Darcy. He didn't have the smarts to get himself out of this. Did he have the stamina? He was young, but all the drugs he'd taken had significantly impaired him.

Tullock cleared his throat. "Is there something I can get you? Water? Coffee?"

"Thanks, but no. I'm good. Where were we?"

"I was telling you about Gaby's abortion."

"Right. Whose baby was it?"

"Park's, probably. My guess is that she and Park didn't want to start a family right away. Although Gaby was raised Catholic, she didn't go to church or confession any more."

I'd been raised Catholic too, but I'd lapsed in my late teens because the Church's actions and attitudes no longer made any sense to me. Over the years I've achieved a certain faith, one that's centered in doing the most good for and the least harm to others. Unfortunately, putting that into practice hasn't always worked as well as I'd've liked.

"This woman who called you," I said, "has a large amount of information about Gaby's private life. Are you sure her voice didn't sound familiar?"

He shook his head.

"And you have no idea who trashed your office at the ranch?"

"No. I don't have any enemies or anything much anybody'd want. And no secrets any more." He glanced at Beth, who smiled faintly.

Secrets, I thought. Most said money was the root of all evil, but in my experience it was secrets—many of them not involving cold, hard cash.

The stupid, harmful things that people do to one another and then feel compelled to cover up. The hidden knowledge that gnaws at them. Such knowledge causes emotional and mental illness and all too often results in violence against the self or others.

Secrets, damned secrets.

# SUNDAY, SEPTEMBER 12

# Mick Savage

As Shar had told him to, he maintained surveillance on the house on Clayton Street. Past midnight the neighborhood was quiet, people returning from Saturday night activities, slotting their cars on an angle on the steep incline. Getting out of cabs. Walking uphill and calling good night to their companions. Lights flared on and winked out. Gradually a middle-of-the-night hush stole over the street.

It was threatening to steal over Mick too, when lights flashed down at the corner and the red Honda pulled into the driveway. The garage door went up and a small figure got out of the car and entered there. The car backed out and drove away.

Mick put on his helmet and fired up the Harley.

The Honda went down the hill and turned right on Oak Street, a conduit to the Central Freeway. Once there, it kept to the right and merged onto 101 South.

*Daly City*, Mick thought. *Peninsula*.

Neither. The Honda veered off onto Alemany Boulevard and into the Excelsior district, an area where a woman he'd once dated lived. The car moved with the slow traffic on Mission Street past an eclectic mix of produce stands, liquor stores, video rental shops, bodegas, check-cashing establishments, and restaurants of every imaginable type. Mick stayed a couple of vehicles back and watched the Honda make a left on Persia Avenue and, several blocks later, drive into McLaren Park.

While McLaren was second only to the Golden Gate in size, for years it had been showing wear and tear. Mick had played baseball there with Alison and some of her buddies from Merrill Lynch, and knew the territory reasonably well. Packed dirt instead of grass, untended recreational areas and playgrounds, lots of litter that often contained discarded needles used by the addicts who frequented the park after the sun fell.

Mick had to follow the Honda with his lights on dim, and he was afraid of hitting a pothole. Fortunately the Honda wasn't going very fast and soon pulled off by an empty parking lot at the base of the Shelley Loop in the north-central area.

He eased his bike into a stand of madrone and killed the engine. An iron pole blocked the entrance to the parking lot, and the Honda idled in front of it. Hadn't the driver known parts of the park were closed from sunset to sunrise?

Mick secured the bike and crept toward the Honda under cover of thick shrubbery. Some kind of plant that grew there made him feel the urge to sneeze, but he choked it back, fingers pinching his nostrils, hand over his mouth.

The car's engine stopped its rumbling, and its lights went out. Seconds later a flash stabbed on. A tall figure skirted the iron pole and the light bobbed ahead of it.

Mick waited a moment, then followed, feeling carefully with his feet over the rough ground. It was cold, and the tall trees were eerie sentinels against the sky—just enough light pollution from the surrounding city to define their trunks and upthrust branches. Then suddenly the torch's bobbing stopped. So did Mick.

The person with the torch was moving it around in ever-widening circles. Searching for something. The light steadied for a moment at one point, angled toward the ground, and before it moved again Mick noted landmarks: three pines formed a triangle, a tangle of vines at its foot. The light turned back his way and he ducked down.

Somebody searching for something that he couldn't look for in daylight.

Behind him the Honda's engine growled, and it rushed past, retracing its route along the Loop road. Impossible to get back to his bike in time to follow, so he slipped ahead through the shrubbery, branches scratching his face and hands, and shone his own light around.

Nothing but a small clearing, and its floor didn't look as if it had been disturbed. When he stepped into it his feet sank a little; he leaned down to feel the ground. Damp, the earth easily scooped up in his hand. Had to be an underground spring here; the park was full of them.

A patch of soft, damp earth not too far from the road in a largely unused area. Given the thickness of the vegetation and lack of a trail, it was unlikely park users would stray into it.

Possible burial spot?

Sudden scrabbling in the bushes behind him. He whirled to see a large figure hurtling forward with an upraised arm. The first blow to his shoulder was glancing, scared the hell out of him. Then he felt a sharp kick on his shin, and when he bent double from the pain the assailant dove at his legs, brought him down. A heavy weight landed on him, drove the air out of his lungs; fists pummeled his face, one jarring blow after another. He couldn't breathe, couldn't move. Blood flowed into his eyes, blurring his vision.

A final blow, and then nothing . . .

# Sharon McCone

It was long after midnight when Hy and I left the Kelowna house, and I was exhausted. This was one of those times when I realized that while I'd come a long way back from being locked in, I still wasn't completely healed. The feeling of being myself, yet not myself, usually filled me with anger, but now I just wanted to cry. I leaned my head against the passenger-side window of our rental car and, face turned away from Hy, let the tears leak. I couldn't fool him: he didn't say anything, but he gave me a squeeze on the shoulder.

*How did I get so lucky?*

"I think I'm good to fly," he said after a few minutes, "if you want to head home tonight."

"You may be good to fly, but your copilot's not." On long trips, it's wise to have somebody alert to spell you in case of a sudden attack of drowsiness.

"So we spend the night under the wing."

"I'd like that."

Sleeping under the wing of the plane is like camping out. Minus the fire and toasted marshmallows or s'mores, on account of the proximity of avgas. We could've spread out on the comfy fold-down seats of this jet, but the idea of cuddling in the double sleeping bag Hy always brought along was more appealing. We drove out to the plane and settled in, and in moments I was out cold.

In the early morning we flew to Sea-Tac, where we passed through customs and took on fuel. And I called Mick but only reached a message center. Puzzled, I called Rae; her phone was off. Ted was at home, though, and glad to hear from me.

"Mick's been hurt," he said. "Happened last night."

"Oh God. How badly? Where is he?"

"Don't panic—he's okay. I talked to him a few minutes ago. He's at UC Med Center. He was mugged in McLaren Park, of all places."

"How serious are his injuries?"

"Scrapes, contusions, a possible concussion, which is why they want to watch him today. No broken bones, no permanent damage."

"What the hell was he doing in McLaren Park at night?"

"Following somebody in a red Honda. He's pretty vague on the details. A couple who were looking for a place to get it on found him crawling along the Shelley Loop and called an ambulance."

The red Honda he'd been tailing earlier last evening. "Did he say anything about Darcy?"

"No."

"What about his assailant?"

"Mick describes him as big and heavy. From the photos I've seen in the files, I gather Darcy's tall and skinny."

"Couldn't have been him anyway. He's not violent."

"Mick was concerned about his bike, so Neal and I are about to go to the park to look for it."

"Well, Hy and I will be on our way home soon. I'll check with you later."

"Saskia, it's not very good news," I said as I watched Hy talking with one of the linemen at the gas pumps.

"I didn't expect good news. Tell me."

That was what I loved about my birth mother: she, like Elwood, accepted—no, wanted—the truth, bad as it might be. Unlike Ma who—God love her—would have wailed and cried and eventually had to be sedated.

"Apparently Darcy's been holed up, alone or with somebody, in a basement apartment in the Haight-Ashbury district. We found the place, but by then he was gone. Later last night Mick was assaulted after tailing a suspect in McLaren Park. It's pretty rough territory, even in daylight, but I've a feeling this was no ordinary mugging. Nothing of Mick's—bike, watch, wallet, phone—was taken."

"Darcy—could he have been the one who attacked Mick?"

"There's no evidence of that."

Saskia sighed. "Sharon, I appreciate what you and Hy are doing. I know you're not . . . fond of Darcy."

"Neither of us really knows him."

"No one does." A touch of bitterness in her tone. "He was such a normal, happy little boy and adolescent, but even then I sensed something different about him." She paused, and I could hear her sucking in her breath. "You're not going to like what I'm about to tell you."

"Try me."

"Thomas Blackhawk was not Darcy's father. I was pregnant by another man when I met Thomas."

Oh, Lord! For a moment I felt light-headed and had to brace myself on the iron fence that separated the general aviation terminal from the field. Ever since Pa died and posthumously led me to the circumstances of my parentage, I'd been barraged with one mind-numbing secret after another.

Surprise: you're adopted! Hello: you've a father in Montana! Welcome: your mother, half sister, and half brother live in Boise!

And now someone else figured into the equation.

I wasn't sure how many more revelations about family matters I could endure.

"Did Thomas know?"

"Yes, I told him, but it didn't make any difference. He always regarded Darcy as his son."

"And the real father?"

"Martin DesChamps."

One of the prominent leaders of the American Indian Movement in the 1980s. He'd been found shot to death in an alley in Denver, roughly eight months before Darcy was born. The case had never been closed.

I asked, "Do you suppose that Darcy's disappearance has something to do with AIM?"

"No, I'd have told you before this if I did. AIM is a prominent force in this country; I've devoted my life to representing them and their causes. But Martin Des-Champs does not reflect the movement as it is today: he was mentally unstable, as many charismatic leaders are. He strayed from the path he'd set out on and destroyed himself in the process."

"But he was murdered—"

"A drug deal gone bad. I've seen the police reports. Some people, when their goals and dreams take a long time to realize, just give in to their worst impulses. I'm afraid Darcy inherited more of his father's genes than mine."

"Does Darcy know who his father was?"

"No. Thomas and I hoped that nurture would triumph over nature. That hope has taken a long time to die, as more and more of his father's craziness came out in him."

"There's no way he could've found out about his father being Martin DesChamps?"

"I don't see how. Other people might've suspected, Robin among them, but Thomas and I were the only ones who knew for sure." She paused. "I've really messed up, haven't I? Giving you up for adoption, lying to Robin and Darcy all their lives."

"You had your reasons. We're a family now."

I saw Hy signaling that he'd finished preflighting. "Got to go, Mom. I'll be in touch."

It was the first time I'd called Saskia Mom.

# Darcy Blackhawk

*Dark, like it's supposed to be when you're dead.*

Cold too. On his back on what felt like concrete. Hands and feet bound. Hands behind him, digging into his spine.

He wiggled around, tried rolling onto his left side. Fell back. Stinging tears flooded his eyes and he lay there, feeling them dribble down his cheeks and into the stubble on his chin. Some of them flowed into his ears and he shook his head back and forth to dislodge them.

He tried to think. Where had he been? Where was he now?

It was a blank, except now he remembered being with Lady Laura.

*"I've just got this one thing to do, Darcy, and then I'll meet you at the Palace.... We'll go someplace nice, like Big Sur."*

He thought he might've been to Big Sur once: tall

trees, cliffs, ocean roar. But that sliver of memory faded fast and left him sad.

Lady Laura, his only friend, and now she was dead. One thing he knew: he hadn't killed her. At first he'd thought he had, but now—in one of those moments his shrinks called "lucid"—he knew she'd been dead when the brown girl had taken him in that taxi to the Palace. What was it the shrinks called taking on guilt for things you didn't do? He couldn't remember.

The tears came faster.

*Not supposed to cry. Men never cry.*

Who'd told him that? Not Dad. Darcy had seen him cry a few times himself. Mom and Robbie also cried: they said it was natural. So who had said men never cry?

Oh yeah, somebody in one of the jails he'd been in. They'd beat the shit out of him.

Jail—that must be where he was now. In jail, in a single cell because they thought he was crazy. In jail where he belonged. But what the hell had he done?

Stolen some waiter's tip off a table at a sidewalk café, he remembered doing that. But nobody'd noticed and the money went as fast as it came. He'd been so hungry....

He should've been hungry now, but his stomach was giving him pains and he felt like he was puffing up.

He used every ounce of strength he had to roll back and forth and finally ended up on his left side. Normally he would've used his hands as a pillow, but they were tied behind him. Why? Cops had never tied his hands before.

*Noisy here*, he thought before he went under. Droning and whining like in a factory. Noisy...

*And dark, like it's supposed to be when you're dead.*

# Sharon McCone

During the flight from Sea-Tac to Oakland, which seemed to take forever, Hy and I discussed what might have happened to Darcy.

"From Mick's description," I said, "that basement apartment where Darcy was staying is pretty squalid. Of course, somebody who'd been living under a bridge might consider it the lap of luxury."

"More likely he wasn't staying there voluntarily."

"You mean he was imprisoned. By the young woman he's been seen with?"

"Possible."

"But why?"

"Could be a kidnapping?"

"Then how come no ransom demand?"

"Money isn't always the primary motivation. A lot of

the cases RI deals with are attempts to gain power, or to force a powerful person into doing what they want."

"The only powerful person connected with Darcy is Saskia. I suppose somebody might want to influence the outcome of one of her pending court cases."

"What's she been working on lately?"

"Nothing terribly exciting, from what she's told me. Actually, she's on a bit of a hiatus, lecturing, writing, and making TV appearances. And even so, you'd think she would've heard something from them by now."

We fell silent and after a time I reviewed my conversation with Jack Tullock. The Gaby DeLucci connection kept coming back to videotapes.

Tapes that Gaby had sent the other Musketeers to get from Drew's house. Tapes that Drew had claimed never existed. Other tapes that someone had ransacked at Drew's house the night before he killed himself. Maybe whoever had gone through his house had found the incriminating ones and threatened to expose him, made monetary demands. Drew would have known that once blackmail begins, it never ends.

Was that another possible reason for his suicide?

Yes, when you considered that Drew's life was very close to ruin. Rumors about his sexual exploitation of Gaby had made the rounds of certain circles for years. His profile on the FreeToHarm site wouldn't go unnoticed by the media and the general populace much longer. Probably the person who had posted the profile was also the blackmailer.

Hy glanced at me. "You want to take the controls?"

"Sure, so long as you keep a close eye on me." It would divert my thoughts from the case for a while and allow the facts to percolate.

The jet flew like a dream. As we entered Bay Area airspace and Hy reclaimed the controls preparatory to our landing at North Field, he said, "You need to get your commercial certification and jet experience."

"Why?"

"Because you're good. And one day this plane may belong to both of us."

"It belongs to RI."

"And who is RI?"

"You, but—"

"And who is McCone Investigations?"

"Me, but—"

He smiled, then spoke to the air traffic controller.

When he was done talking, I said, "Ripinsky, are you proposing a business merger?"

"Would that be such a bad idea?"

"But everything's so good the way it is."

"When have I heard that before? We got married anyway."

"Yes, but marriage—"

"—Is one of the most difficult and risky things most people ever do. By comparison, a business merger is a piece of cake."

"Says you."

"Think about it, McCone. That's all I'm asking."

At UC Med Center on Parnassus Heights I chanced to meet Rae in one of the elevators. "Prepare yourself," she said. "Mick's in a foul mood."

"Uh-oh."

"His head, he says, feels like it's been run over by a tractor in a newly fertilized field. His breakfast was like porridge the Three Bears wouldn't've eaten. The nurse would be a pit bull if she was shorter and had four legs."

"I never knew he could come up with such colorful images."

"Neither did Alison. She visited earlier and he told her that her father—you remember he came out from Indiana for a few days last month—reminded him of a troll."

"Jesus!"

Rae smiled wryly. "Fortunately, Alison thinks so too."

We'd reached Mick's room. "There're two other patients in there with him," Rae added. "One reads *The Wall Street Journal*, keeps his headphones on, and watches FOX News. The other, I think, is in a coma. They're all separated by those curtains that pull around the bed, thank God."

I remembered hospital rooms only too well. Even being here made my palms sweat.

Rae held up a grease-stained paper bag. "Señor Loco's burrito grande."

"Do they let them have that stuff here?"

"They'd better, or the Pit Bull will die in a patient uprising. You want to give it to him?"

"No. I want to talk with him, and I'd rather not do it when he's got guacamole dribbling from his lips."

"...Right. I'll ask the nurse to keep it warm."

Mick's was the middle bed. I pulled the curtain aside and at first thought he was asleep. Then he turned fierce blue eyes on me.

"My head hurts like hell, and the food's bad enough to make a Dumpster diver puke."

"Good morning to you too." I sat down on the foot of the bed.

"Alison was here. She wants me to move into her place after I get out so she can treat me like an invalid."

"I'm sure she has your best interests in mind."

"They all do. That's how they get you."

Mick, I was sure, had never been "gotten" by a woman in his life. In fact, he seemed to have worked on losing them.

"Rae came," he added, "and I asked her to get me some Señor Loco. Where the hell is she?"

I didn't reply, just looked at him.

Under the thin hospital sheet and blanket he squirmed, a flush spreading from his neck to his face. He turned his head to the side.

"Must sound pretty lame to you," he said. "These complaints, I mean."

"I know how helpless you feel."

"Not as helpless as you were last year."

"It's all a matter of degree. Do you feel like talking about what happened to you?"

"Not till I get my burrito."

I sighed and went to find Rae.

The food worked wonders on Mick.

"Nothing like a burrito to perk a guy up," he said.

"If that were true of every guy, we'd have world peace." I sat on the visitor's chair. "So what d'you remember about last night?"

"I was tailing that red Honda I told you about. The driver was the only one in it as far as I could tell. He drove into McLaren Park and stopped on the Shelley Loop. I followed him to a clearing in a deep thicket, where he looked around with a flashlight. Then he got out of there so fast I couldn't get back to my bike in time to keep tailing him, so I went back to the clearing. Nothing but soft ground, probably from one of those underground springs. I had the feeling he was scoping out a place to bury a body."

"Not good. Are you sure it was a man?"

"Pretty much; he was big. Like the guy who jumped me."

"You get a look at him?"

"Practically none at all."

"What did you hear before he attacked you?"

"Thrashing in the thicket. Heavy footsteps. I think he was wearing pointy-toed boots."

"Why?"

"Felt like it when he kicked me."

"Anything else about him? An odor?"

"Sweat. Leather. Old leather, not that new-car smell. A jacket, maybe."

"You make a good witness, Savage, even if you were getting the shit kicked out of you."

"I'll treasure the compliment forever," he said. "Now how about getting out of here so I can rest."

I was waiting at the elevator when my phone rang. An unfamiliar male voice said, "We have your brother Darcy."

"What? Who is this?"

"Never mind that. We *have* him, and if you want him back alive, you better follow instructions."

So Hy had been right. Quickly I turned up the volume on the phone as high as it would go, rummaged in my bag for my tape recorder, and began documenting the call.

"Is Darcy all right?"

"He's alive. He'll remain alive as long as you do as we say."

"What do you want me to do?"

"We'll negotiate this in stages. If at any time you contact the authorities, the negotiations will stop. And your brother will die." The voice sounded as if he was distorting it with some device. "Your first step is to gather fifty thousand dollars in small bills, no larger than twenties. You have until seven tonight."

"Fifty thousand—it's Sunday!"

"Like I said, you have until seven tonight. Do it." He broke the connection.

Immediately I speed-dialed Hy and explained that there'd been a ransom demand after all.

He said, "I'm not too surprised. Whatever these people had in mind with Darcy at first must not have worked out, so they've shifted to a fallback position. That's why there's been no ransom demand until now."

"How should we handle it?"

"My advice is to follow the caller's instructions to the letter. Tell no one else about this."

"But the money—"

"I have ways of getting it, even on a Sunday. Ransom demands don't always come during banking hours, you know. RI will manage this as we always do."

# Mick Savage

He'd insisted Alison bring his laptop to the hospital, and after Shar left and he'd rested awhile he went to work.

The license plates on the red Honda he'd tailed to McLaren Park belonged to a black Mercedes that had been junked behind a business on Edgewater Road in Oakland two months ago. The car had been stolen off a dealer's lot in Santa Rosa. The Honda itself was registered to a Kay Zimmerman of Prairie Village, Kansas; she'd reported it stolen six months ago. Given the fact that she was a respected faculty member at the University of Kansas, it followed that she was not moonlighting as a kidnapper in California.

He then called Real Good Properties, the management company that had leased the apartments in the Clayton Street house; its office was open on Sunday, as most realty offices were. Cyndi Smith—who emphasized the spelling of her first name—was initially reluctant to give out details on the tenants, but Mick charmed her with a description of his credentials, which somehow worked as an aphrodisiac on certain young women.

The Bartletts on three had lived in their apartment for seven years. Good tenants, paid their rent on time. Ed Moss and his wife, Lucinda, on two, were much the same. And the Morgans on one, although they had been there only a few months, were turning out to be model renters. The basement apartment? Well, that had always been a problem.

How so? Mick asked.

It seemed to attract all kinds of lowlifes, Cyndi told him. There had been multiple complaints from the other residents and her firm had prepared eviction notices at least five times since she'd been employed there. All the tenants served with notices had fled leaving debris, damage, and overdue rent. After the last couple had trashed the bathroom, the owners had decided to take the basement apartment off the market.

Who were the owners? Mick asked.

Oh, one of those partnerships in Culver City down south that bought up marginal properties and used them as a tax write-off. Janus Corporation. They'd recently filed for bankruptcy.

No way he'd reach anyone connected with them on a Sunday. Besides, he was getting sleepy.

When Alison came into the room, carrying a covered basket from which the aromas of their favorite Thai restaurant emanated, his memory was drawn back to the morning last year when she'd shown up at the pier with a similar basket of breakfast goodies for everybody, because she knew they'd had a bad night.

"Hungry?" she asked.

"Ravenous." The burrito was just a distant memory now.

She removed cartons from the basket, pulled out paper plates and plastic forks. "No chopsticks," she said. "Too sloppy for hospitals." A warmth spread throughout his chest. He supposed, from his limited knowledge, that it was love.

*Don't lose this one, Savage.* **Marry** *her.*

# Darcy Blackhawk

*Where am I?*

Not in jail. He knew that much.

It was still dark. Earlier this place had been noisy, but now the droning and whining were spaced out and distant. His hands and feet were still tied, but not as tightly as before. Had they moved him?

He remembered somebody coming in, roughly moving him aside. For a few minutes they squatted in the far corner, doing something with the help of a flashlight. After they were gone he felt the temperature rising, enough to take the chill off his bones.

He'd told somebody something at one point. Who? The brown girl? What?

A lie, to make them stop hurting him. A lie that would be bad for Shar. But what was it?

He'd said...said that...

Oh, shit. Why couldn't he remember? Why wasn't he like other people?

His eyes stung. No, he wasn't going to cry again. He'd think about what he'd told them. . . .

Now he remembered. He'd said that Shar had the box Lady Laura had given him. Only she didn't, because Laura hadn't given him anything except a little snort of coke. He'd been so glad to see her, and she'd promised to meet him at some palace later. Then they'd go away, start a new life in Big Sur. But first there was something she had to do.

She hadn't told him what, and now she was dead.

Why *was* Lady Laura dead?

Darcy's head ached. Drug hangover, the kind that you had when the docs pumped too many meds into you. That shrink, the time he'd freaked out and ended up in the psych ward in Boise. The other time too, someplace in Oregon.

There'd been needle marks on his arm this time, he'd seen them.

Why hadn't they just killed him? It would've been better for Shar that way. Better for everybody. If he could ever get out of here, he'd do the job himself.

Here. Where was here?

*Where am I?*

# Sharon McCone

Hy set a battered brown briefcase on my desk at the pier and sat across from me.

"It's all there," he said. "Unmarked bills, although the serial numbers have been recorded and will be circularized. But most kidnappers know that's standard procedure; they'll launder it."

"In your experience, isn't fifty thousand kind of small for a ransom demand?"

"Yes, but remember that the clients RI deals with are high-profit multinational corporations."

"So these people could be amateurs."

"Could be, or maybe they've done their homework—credit reports, that kind of stuff—and know what the traffic will bear."

I shifted in my chair, put my feet up on the pullout shelf of my workstation. My body tingled with excess adrenaline. "You planning to make the drop? I mean, it's your area of expertise."

"I'm not planning anything. We'll do as they say. Cardinal rule of ransom situations. But don't worry, I'll be here every step of the way. And once the kidnapper has the briefcase, there's a microchip in its lining that will transmit a signal to a device I can link to my GPS, so I can track him."

Hy knew exactly what to do. For twenty years he had been a skillful hostage negotiator; when he took over RI, he'd kept on top of all the new technology, hired the best people in the necessary areas of expertise. Now RI was the best in the field of international executive protection and security.

It wasn't yet seven o'clock, but I had my phone out and was primed for it to ring.

Hy saw me glance at it and said, "They usually delay the call. Puts you on edge, makes you more compliant. Try not to come off that way when the call comes; it'll confuse them and we'll have an advantage."

I nodded, but kept looking at the phone.

"You let Saskia or Robin know what's going on?" he asked.

"God, no. The man on the phone said to tell no one, and besides, I don't want to put them through this."

"Good. You hungry?"

"I'd choke on so much as a sip of water."

The phone rang, and I reached for it.

Hy put his hand over mine. "Deep breath before you answer."

I breathed, then picked up. It was Ma: the replacement for the pair of pink slippers was on its way. I gave Hy a what-do-I-do-now? look.

He leaned forward, took the phone. "Hi, Kay. I'm about to whisk your daughter off for a romantic dinner, and if we don't go now we'll lose our reservation. Can you and she talk about the slippers in the morning?...Right, a popular restaurant, and they don't hold your place more than five minutes....Okay, I'll tell her. And you have a nice evening." He handed the cellular back to me.

"She sends her love," he said.

"Why didn't I check to see who was calling before I answered?"

"You're overanxious. Let's just relax."

We lapsed into silence. Around us the old pier creaked and groaned, and above us traffic on the Bay Bridge rattled and roared.

Again it was silent. Then Hy asked, "You heard any more from the port commission?"

"No. Glenn Solomon's been keeping tabs on the situation and he says the outlook isn't promising. This city—it's tearing everything down. Granted, the Transbay Terminal wasn't viable any more, but still the demolition made me sad."

The terminal was built in 1939 as a hub for the Key System trains from the East Bay and, later, for buses. It had been torn down last year. I remembered it well from all the times during college when I'd passed through on my way between Berkeley and my security guard jobs in the city. Even then it had been a characterless dingy gray building—its restaurants, the well-known Cuddles Bar, and the shoeshine stands long closed and sealed off from the public. Then the police station, with its conveniently located drunk tank, went dark too. The homeless took over, and the lobby and corridors smelled of urine and strong disinfectant.

Now it had temporarily been replaced by eleven white vinyl canopies that stretched over a concrete plaza like giant umbrellas; to many people's surprise, they were not as ugly or inconvenient as many of us had thought they would be. By 2017 they would be permanently replaced by a $910 million transit hub, and the Bay Area would eventually expand to previously undreamed-of limits.

Progress, yes. But progress is not always good, and sometimes I have dark thoughts of California's becoming nothing more than one sanitized unending city from border to border. Then, of course, I think of the Sierras and the other mountain chains, as well as the fertile central valleys—millions of acres of farmland that grow produce that feeds the whole country's population. Too valuable to be turned into housing developments and shopping malls; the land will be there long after the cities self-destruct.

Hy said, "I could see the demolition of the terminal from my office windows. Made me a little sad too." RI was located on the nineteenth floor of a new building on Battery Street. "Some columnist in the *Chron* was carrying on a while back about how San Franciscans resist change for no good reason."

"There's a little bit of truth in that, but I think it's more that we revere tradition. We have a fabulous history here, and it would be a shame for it to be wiped out. We've already got the Transamerica Pyramid, Embarcadero Center, Millennium Tower, and some pretty ugly public art. What more do we need?"

"I don't much like public art. A buddy of mine in Los Alegres says there's a truly hideous ice-cream cone statue in front of the cinemaplex. And, of course, there's that obelisk made out of bicycle parts in Santa Rosa." Hy paused. "If the pier really is demolished, have you given any more thought to where you'll relocate?"

"I should have, but since Darcy disappeared I haven't had the time or inclination. Ted's on the hunt, though. The Grand Poobah says he won't let us move into an ordinary office building. He's got his heart set on someplace more unique."

"Where?"

"Tel Hill near Pioneer Park."

"Tel Hill! More like Parking Hell."

"The building has an underground garage that holds a dozen cars. And an elevator."

"What else?"

"Ted says it's narrow, four stories, and painted blue, slate blue. His favorite color. It's been vacant for over a year. We could negotiate a really favorable long-term lease."

"Why's it been vacant?"

"Um...that's kind of unpleasant—"

The sudden sound of my phone ringing made me jump.

"Deep breath," Hy warned.

The voice on the line was the one I'd heard before: male, with a tinny, distorted quality. He spoke fast, giving me no time to interrupt him or to form an impression of what kind of man I was dealing with. There was a pronounced click when he ended the call.

I said to Hy, "Here's what's happening: he wants me to make the drop at Elk Glen Lake in the park."

"Where Gaby DeLucci's body was found."

"To the exact spot."

Hy's eyes darkened. "Does he think that's funny? Or ironic?"

"Who knows?"

"When does he want you there?"

"Eleven-thirty."

"The same time Gaby's body was found. I don't like this, McCone. Whoever he is, he's toying with you."

"I know. But he's also doing himself a disservice: he's given us time to go over maps of the area, plan surveillance and escape routes—both his and ours. We'd better get started."

# Darcy Blackhawk

*Maybe I'm dead.*

It was dark and he was cold. Couldn't feel his fingers or feet any more. Couldn't hear anything except for a whining in the distance.

No, not dead. He was breathing. When he blinked, his eyelids rasped against his eyeballs. And he could feel his heart beating.

That awful, stinking room. The girl hurting him. Needle marks, pain, and then nothing else until...a car.

He was in a car. The tires were thrumming over smooth pavement. What car? No memory.

Okay, maybe if he tried real hard he could remember that day when he'd met the girl.

Lady Laura had something to do with it. Oh, yeah, she'd been with the girl on that street. Laura'd told him they needed money. The girl asked where the tapes were. What tapes? he said. The ones Laura gave you, she replied. We can make plenty of money with those.

He'd glanced at Laura, and she gave him one of her looks: he'd always been able to figure out what those looks meant; she wanted him to act crazy. So he mumbled and shifted from foot to foot and scratched his head.

Laura said, "He could do with a fix. So could I."

The brown girl led them around the corner, into an alley between an auto body repair and an empty storefront. He and Laura had a couple of snorts, and the girl gave Laura the rest of what was in the baggie.

"Now," she said, "the tapes."

Laura was slinking off down the alley. She'd told him she'd meet him later at the palace. He needed help.

*McConeInvestigations.com.*

It just popped into his head, the way stuff did now and then.

Down the street he'd seen an Internet café. And he remembered Mom's password. He'd used it before, to get online and buy stuff with her credit card.

"I'll show you," he said.

The Wiring Hall. Through its front window he saw its free terminals.

"Let me go in first. They know me."

He went inside and straight to the closest terminal. Fired off a message to Shar. Pressed the Send button just before the girl grabbed his arm and dragged him outside.

"What the hell have you done?" she demanded.

"Nothing."

"Like hell! Where are those tapes?"

He remembered something Laura had told him, on one of those soft nights by the Salmon River.

"Gaby is dead and buried under a coral tree." Then he added, "I need to go to the palace to meet Laura."

So she'd taken him to this big round place with pillars near a lake, but Laura wasn't there.

Except she was.

Jesus God her dead face. How could he have done that to her?

Next the girl took him to a big stone museum. Made him ask where the cemetery was.

They'd driven to an old, weedy cemetery somewhere south of the city. Sad little gravestone tucked off by itself. The name on the marker was of the woman Laura had told him about.

"Are the tapes here?" the girl asked.

He'd shaken his head, but all the same he'd whispered a prayer over the gravestone, twisting the straw so he'd stay calm.

"Look, you know where those tapes are! You're going to tell me."

He looked down at his hands. Straw. Where had that come from?

The girl said, "Gaby would want me to have them. Tell me where they are."

He dropped the straw. "I'm sick," he said. "I'm hungry. I can't think."

"You better think, damn you!"

That was the beginning of his nightmare.

*Stop! You're hurting me!*

Somebody was dragging him. Thumping him over the

ground, jarring his spine. His head hurt more than it ever had in his life.

He moaned.

A man's voice said, "Shut up."

He knew that voice. The man had been in the tall house.

"Who are—?"

"Shut up!"

*But you're hurting me!*

*I want to go home.*

Wherever that was, he wanted to be there. With Mom. With Dad—no, he was dead. With Robbie—no, Robbie hated him. With Shar, only she probably hated him too.

He didn't want to go home to the river any more. Forget the soft nights, the stars, the rippling waters, the great dope. That had all turned to shit when the law came. He didn't want to go home to Laura and all those crappy rat-infested places where they'd hidden afterward from the rain and the cold. Couldn't do that anyway—Laura was dead. And he never wanted to see the little brown girl who he'd thought he loved till she'd started her angry questions and her hitting and kicking and stabbing him full of drugs.

There was nobody, no place, but he still wanted to go home.

A noise overhead. Coming closer, lower. Jesus, what was *that*?

Something big and loud roared over wherever he was.

Airplane. Right overhead. Got to get out of here!

He doubled over, began biting at the duct tape that bound his ankles. His right eyetooth came out. Blood poured into his mouth, over his stubbled chin. He ignored the pain, kept biting.

Soon his mouth and chin were slick with blood. He flopped onto his back, heart pounding. All that work for nothing, and now the drugs were doing *their* work. One of those shrinks, wherever he'd been, had told him about how drugs stayed inside your system, could get whipped up into a frenzy for no reason at all.

Well, they were frenzied now, and there wasn't anything he could do about it but wait them out, unless...

*Maybe I'm dead.*

# Sharon McCone

Familiar places are transformed by darkness. I'd been to Elk Glen Lake in Golden Gate Park numerous times for picnics or just to sit and watch the ducks glide on its placid, grayish-green water. Although it's not all that far from the Twenty-fifth Avenue entrance to the park and Martin Luther King Boulevard, the surrounding high grasses and trees—cherry, plum, and willow, as well as pine—provide a peaceful haven and the lake has relatively few visitors. It's listed on a website as one of the best places to make love outdoors in the city. In fact, Hy and I had once done just that under the pines on its shore.

Tonight, however, I felt as if I were entering an alien landscape—remote, empty, full of restless shadows. The full moon silvered the lawn on the slope leading down to the water, made it look icy and slippery. The nighttime temperature was in the forties, too cold for the light jacket

I'd worn for the sunny day. I stood at the top of the slope, contemplating what we'd decided to be the best way down there.

Hy was nearby, under cover of the trees. He'd parked on Lincoln Way, presuming the kidnapper would also do so because it was a short distance to the lake through deserted territory. On the other hand, I'd left my car on Martin Luther King, hoping the bright moonlight would allow the kidnapper to see me clearly—to see that I had the old briefcase in my bandaged left hand. Would be so riveted by it that even if he noticed my right hand tucked in my jacket's slash pocket, he would think it was for warmth and not because it was resting on my .357 Magnum.

I moved down the slope slowly, as Hy and I had planned, giving both him and the kidnapper plenty of time to spot me. Paused to orient myself and to listen before I followed the route we'd mapped out through the trees. Night whispers: the cry of a bird and the rustlings of small nocturnal animals. Traffic thrumming nearby, but muted.

To my right a twig snapped. I turned my head, peered into the darkness. The kidnapper wouldn't be so stupid as to try to grab me before I made the drop, would he? Well, he might. Better get going.

I was to follow the dirt path around the lake to a large flat rock on the reedy shoreline where Gaby had been found. Place the briefcase into a cavity under the rock, then retrace my route to my car. Afterward there was no telling what might happen. As a precaution I planned to make a more circuitous, confusing retreat.

I took out my pencil flash and started around the lake. It was rough going: pine branches slapped me on the head no matter how low I ducked. Roots protruding from the soft soil threatened to trip me; blackberry vines grabbed at my ankles. High in the trees an owl hooted, and was answered by another.

My foot slipped on a slick patch and I went down on one knee, smearing mud on my jeans. Pushed up—more mud on my hand. I wiped it off and kept going, taking smaller, more cautious steps.

Another twig snapped. I wanted to drop the briefcase and run, had to remind myself to follow my instructions. Hy had drummed that into me as we planned: "No deviations. I'll be there if you need me."

I could see the rock now—granite, smooth, with small flaring sparkles. The moonlight shone directly on it, but unlike on the lawn it revealed only a stark ugliness.

Did places take on an aura from events that happened there?

I'd always believed so.

I could imagine a similar moonlit night. A dark shape carrying a slight, limp form through the trees. He would've left his vehicle on MLK Boulevard—too much traffic on Twenty-fifth Avenue—and returned to it by the same hidden route as soon as he'd dumped his burden, never suspecting it would be discovered within hours.

The autopsy report said that Gaby had died between seven and eight that evening, results based on stomach contents, a meal she'd had around two that afternoon. Ravioli and a green salad, at a café on Union Street. She'd been with another woman, and they'd laughed a lot, their waiter said, before they'd left at a little after three. The police traced the woman, who turned out to be an acquaintance from boarding school, and had quickly been cleared of any involvement in the murder. That time frame gave Gaby's killer plenty of time to dispose of her body and to establish an effective alibi.

I moved closer to the rock, clutching the briefcase. No sounds except those of fish occasionally slapping the water. My senses were high-tuned, humming. I scanned the surrounding terrain, saw no sign of anyone. When I reached the rock I took a final look around and then shoved the briefcase under it. Made my zigzag retreat through the underbrush to my car.

Nothing happened on the way. I started the engine and drove away.

Soon, thinking he was alone, the kidnapper would go for the briefcase. Then Hy would take over.

It had all gone according to plan because of Hy's expertise, developed over years of hostage negotiation. I owed him—for this and so much more.

# MONDAY, SEPTEMBER 13

# Sharon McCone

Hy checked in by phone at half past twelve as I drove back toward the pier.

"The guy went straight to his car on Lincoln Way. Took his time making a U-turn, so I was able to catch up with him. He's heading west on Lincoln Way. We're almost to the Great Highway."

"Have you gotten a look at who's driving?"

"Nope. Traffic's light, so I'm keeping my distance."

"Well, keep me posted."

As soon as I clicked off, the speakerphone buzzed again. Mick.

"You're supposed to be resting," I said.

"I am, under the sheets with my laptop, like I used to do with a book and a flashlight when I was a kid. The nurse—new, cute one—is onto me, but so far she's been lenient. Anyway, I've been checking the FAA sites like you suggested. One of the planes owned by Bellassis Aviation left SFO for Portland at eleven-forty p.m. on September eighth, returned around nine the next morning."

"Quick trip."

"Very. It was a Citation, like the ones Hy's company owns."

"And the pilot?"

"One of the owners of the FBO—Lucy Bellassis."

Lucy?

*"And you, Lucy, I believe you said you fly too?"*

*"Some. My license is current, but I prefer to limit myself to the right seat."*

*"My little copilot."*

Park had said that sardonically, not as a literal statement. She didn't confine herself to the copilot's seat and she hadn't mentioned what ratings she had or what kind of aircraft she'd been checked out in. She hadn't mentioned piloting the jet.

We'd been putting on the same act Wednesday night— slightly ditzy, oh-little-me—and neither of us had recognized it in the other.

"See if you can find out what she did in the Portland area," I said—although I already had a strong suspicion.

Hy checked in again as I changed my course toward Sea Cliff. "Honda's merged onto Skyline. It could go south to San Jose or double back to the city. You at the pier yet?"

"No. I'm going to the Bellassises'."

"New development?"

"I'll tell you about it later."

The fog had held off far out on the horizon all day and evening but now, after one in the morning, it was filtering in, obscuring the moon and stars. The Sea Cliff neighborhood was so socked in that I had to turn my fog lights on bright, and even then I strained to see the curbs and parked cars. A few dimly lit shapes of windows appeared and disappeared.

It was a long time before Lucy's nervous voice called out from behind the door. "Who is it?"

I glanced up at where I'd previously noticed a surveillance camera; its red light was off. "Sharon McCone."

"Oh God, you scared me! Park's away, and all of the help are off tonight." There was a rattling noise, and then she opened the door. Her tall, thin frame was wrapped in an elegantly styled silk robe that matched her gray eyes; incongruously, on her feet she wore orange-and-black-striped plush slippers fashioned to look like tigers' heads, complete with bared plastic fangs.

They reminded me of Ma's recent gift that was traveling around the family. Sure as hell those pink slippers looked like bunny rabbits. I hoped whichever of my siblings next received them would throw them out before they got to me.

Lucy saw me staring at her feet. "Park's idea of a joke—he calls me his 'little tiger.'"

"And his 'little copilot.'"

"Oh, well…" She hesitated. "Come in."

I stepped inside. "Did you know your security system's off?"

"Damn!" She punched at the keypad.

"Where's Park tonight? Out of town again?"

"Supposedly at the FBO. He claimed he was in a hurry to take a package of documents we had notarized late this afternoon out to the airport to one of their couriers."

"What kind of documents?"

"Business stuff. I don't know." She shifted slightly, put out a hand to steady herself against the wall.

"Didn't you even read the documents' titles?"

"God, Sharon, what does it matter? Look, I need another drink. You want to have one with me?"

"I'm working, Lucy. And I don't think you understand the seriousness of this situation. What do you remember of the documents?"

"Nothing. It doesn't matter."

Yes, it did. I suspected Park had gotten her to sign off on as many of their joint assets as possible. But why? He had everything he wanted, including a rich wife.

"You say there was a notary here?"

"Yeah."

"His or her name?"

"I don't know."

"Male? Female?"

"Female."

"Did she leave you her card?"

"No. Park might have it. Or maybe Torrey."

"Torrey was here too?"

"The notary was a friend of hers, I think."

I closed and chained the door behind me and followed her into the living room.

"You sure you don't want a drink?" Lucy asked.

"You have any ginger ale?"

"No ginger ale," Lucy said. "But if you're into a soft drink, how about Coke with a touch of rum?"

"Okay, fine."

I surveyed the big luxurious room and its comfortable furnishings. All seemed as they had before, except for a broken-spined paperback romance novel on a side table.

"Lucy," I said, "what time did Park leave?"

"Nine? Nine-thirty? I don't remember exactly."

I followed her into the living room to the bar. Lucy turned to me—a rigid, too-bright smile on her face and icy fear in her eyes. Her gaze was doing funny things—jumping from side to side, up and down, in a random order.

"Here's your rum and Coke," she said. Her hand shook as she gave it to me.

No ice, and very little Coke. Strong odor of rum, a liquor I don't particularly like.

"Let's sit down," I said.

"I can't. I'm too nervous."

"Why? What're you so afraid of?"

She shook her head.

"Something Park did?"

Silence.

"Something Park's going to do?"

No response. Her right hand was twisting at her diamond wedding band.

"Well, if you don't want to talk about that, let's talk about why you flew to Portland and ransacked Jack Tullock's place."

She blinked at me. "How do you know about that?"

"FAA records. If you didn't want to be found out, you shouldn't have filed a flight plan."

"That's me," she said bitterly. "The good little girl who always plays by the rules. But at the time I hadn't done anything wrong, so I didn't feel the need for secrecy."

"Why did you go there?"

"After you showed me the photo you found of the Four Musketeers, I called Mr. Tullock to ask if he had any other pictures of the group that might shed some light on

Gaby's murder. There was no answer. I thought by the time I got there he'd be at home. So I went right away."

"Why the hurry?"

"Why not? When your best friend's murdered and nobody's doing anything about it any more, if there's a possibility you can, you grab on to it."

"So you got up there...?"

"And when I called from the airport, there was no answer again. So I used one of the FBO's vans and drove to his ranch. Still nobody, but the house and his office were unlocked. I know I shouldn't have gone in and searched, but by then I was so worked up. I broke a vase in the house, and I made a terrible mess in the studio. I didn't mean to, but I was afraid they'd come back and find me. And there were all these weird noises outside."

Jack Tullock's exotic animals.

"I found something too," Lucy added. "Not what I wanted or expected. It...I'll show you." She left the room, returned with a faded color photograph. "It's time- and date-stamped. Taken at Wildside, a bar where they all used to hang out."

The bar where Tullock claimed he'd gotten blind drunk the night he was supposed to kill Clarence Drew. Apparently not so drunk that he couldn't take photographs.

The picture showed Park in profile, slouching at a table with a row of empty glasses in front of him. A blond woman, her hair a mass of long curls, sat next to him, holding his hand.

Lucy's sister, Torrey.

"Did you know this was going on?" I asked, tapping the image of her sister.

"Not at the time, no."

"When did you find out?"

"A couple of months ago. Torrey had come over to use Park's computer. She was always doing that. And I heard them talking."

"Park was involved with your sister back then, but he was planning to marry Gaby anyway?"

"Yes, so he could get hold of her money. When she was killed, he exaggerated his grief and went after me."

"Why not Torrey, since they were already involved?"

She sat down and seemed to shrink in the big chair. "Because Torrey's unstable, not suitable as a wife. And my parents have written her out of their will. Me, I'm pliable, I can be what he needs. I stand to inherit, and my father made Park a big loan to expand the chain of FBOs. But there's something about Torrey's instability that excites Park like I never have."

She seemed to listen to her words. "Well, I'm not pliable any more," she added. "Not any more."

I asked Lucy if I could take a look at Park's computer. She led me upstairs into a sparsely furnished office—just a computer, printer, and scanner.

"I don't know anything about these machines," Lucy said. "I hope you do."

The computer was an iMac like mine. I reached around its back and turned it on, hoping Park had stored his password. He had, and why not? Lucy wouldn't have known how to use it. I clicked Mail, found all the boxes were empty. There were few desktop icons and none of interest.

Park's browser was Firefox. I opened it, clicked History, scrolled down, selected the entries for the past two months. And there was my answer.

Repeated postings on FreeToHarm.com. Postings that had probably prompted Clarence Drew to kill himself.

Had Park posted them? No, he might cheat his wife out of her portion of their joint assets, but this was not his style. Whose, then? The woman Clarence Drew had thrown out of his house the day before he killed himself?

I checked the last posting on FreeToHarm; it was from noon of the day Drew hanged himself.

My cell rang. Mick again.

"Two things," he said. "Laura Mercer first. She was in the county lockup on charges of possession of cocaine. Her cellmate was Torrey Grant, Lucy Bellassis's sister. I spoke with one of the guards there. After a lot of lucrative promises on my part he told me the two got very friendly. In fact, they appeared to be exchanging life stories."

"Were they released at the same time?"

"No. Torrey ten days before Laura."

But they could have arranged to meet when Laura got out.

"Okay. What's the other thing?"

"I just sent a picture to your cell phone. I took it inside the house on Clayton, but with the attack and the drugs and all, I forgot about it till now."

I said, "Wait a minute," and put him on hold. Brought up the photo. It was actually a picture of a picture.

Torrey Grant and Jeff Morgan.

Although I recognized the pair, I showed the picture to Lucy for confirmation. "Yes, that's my sister and Jeff," she said. "Where'd you get this?"

"No time to explain now. What's their address?"

It was the house on Clayton Street.

*    *    *

"You going to be okay?" I asked Lucy on my way out.

"Of course. The alarm's on. And Park's not coming back."

"Are you sure of that?"

"Yes. He's got what he wants—he thinks."

"What does that mean?"

A sly smile spread across her face. "The signed quit-claims on our properties and business and transfers of our investment accounts. Only they're not going to do him any good. I may come across as a fluffy, no-brain twen-tysomething, and I've acted the part because it was what Park wanted. But tonight he said he was in a hurry to get those documents signed, so they could go off with a cou-rier. That was a bit of nonsense: property transfers have to be taken to the county clerks, and changes in owner-ship submitted to the various investment institutions. He's probably holing up at our Napa Valley house with one of his sweeties until start of business tomorrow."

I sensed what was coming. "What did you do?"

"Deviated from my usual handwriting—just a little bit so he wouldn't notice—and misspelled my last name. Instead of Bellassis, I wrote B-e-l-a-s-s-e-s. Knowing Park as I do, I was sure he wouldn't even glance at the signatures. He didn't, and he won't until he tries to use them."

Lights were on behind closed draperies of the first-floor apartment of the house on Clayton. I knocked, and Tor-rey's voice called out, "Jeff, it's about time. What took you so long?"

When she opened the door and saw me, a mixture of

dismay and fear clouded her features. "You," she said flatly, and tried to slam the door. I blocked it with my foot and shoulder. Behind her I could see a row of mismatched suitcases.

"Jeff's not coming." As I'd driven here from Sea Cliff, Hy had checked in to say that the red Honda was bypassing San Jose and heading west.

"What? How do you—?"

"Where's Darcy?"

"...Who?"

"My brother Darcy. What've you and Morgan done with him?"

I pushed through the door, forcing her to back up. Her face had gone pale, the fright sharp in her eyes.

"I don't know what you're talking about."

I made a menacing move toward her, and she shrank back against the wall. "Where is he?"

"I...I don't know."

"No good, Torrey. You know, all right. And don't bother trying to cover for Morgan. My agency's been tailing him ever since he picked up the ransom money at the park. My last report was that he's now headed west of San Jose. He cut you out of the deal."

"You're lying!"

"You haven't heard from him, have you?"

She gave me a defiant look, then whirled suddenly and ran down the hallway. I sprinted after, had no trouble grabbing her shoulders and bringing her down on the threshold of the kitchen. She struggled for a moment, then went still. She was a nasty piece of work, but a fighter she wasn't.

"Where's Darcy? Is he still alive?"

"... Yeah, I think so."

"You think so. He'd better be. If anything happens to him, you'll be facing lethal injection right along with Morgan."

Torrey moaned, a self-pitying sound. "I wasn't there when he killed that old drunk out at the projects. That was his idea. He wanted to kill Darcy too, but I wouldn't let him...."

There wasn't time to get the rest of the story out of her, but I figured out most of it anyway. The details would come later. The important thing now was to find Darcy.

"Once more, damn you: WHERE IS HE?"

Dully: "Jeff had him stashed someplace at the FBO. I guess he's still there."

I pushed up to my feet, hurried down the hallway. As soon as I was out of the building Torrey would go on the run. But she wouldn't get far. I knew it and she knew it, but that wouldn't stop her from making the effort.

Losers like her keep on being losers to the very end.

On my way to SFO I called Hy. "Where are you?"

"Halfway to Santa Cruz."

"Do you have an operative in the area who can take over for you? I need you up here."

He recognized the urgency in my voice and didn't ask why. "Hold on." A minute later he came back. "Op named Zoe Wasler lives five minutes from where I am. We'll meet up, I'll give her the tracking device, then I'll head back."

"I'll meet you at SFO. You hooked in with anybody in security there?"

"Go-to man this time of morning is Dave Homestead.

I'll get onto him and let you know where to meet us. You can fill me in on what's happening then."

Dave Homestead was tall and bald with a roughly hewn face and blue eyes that crackled with intensity. I doubted he smiled much—if ever. Hy and I met with him and two of his colleagues in a conference room upstairs in the international terminal, where I laid out Lucy Bellassis's story.

One of the colleagues went over and pulled down a map of the airport. It was constructed on a crisscross pattern—dual runways from northwest to southeast, a second, shorter pair from northeast to southwest. The terminals were northeast of the longest runway, 10L.

"This," he said, pointing to an area to the northwest of the main double runways, "is general aviation. And this"—a few inches to the left—"is the Bellassis FBO."

I waited impatiently.

Homestead took over. "You say Park Bellassis's wife thinks your brother is being held in the facility itself, but I doubt that. Too many people coming and going, plus the building is designed in such a way it would be extremely difficult to conceal someone who was being confined against his will."

Having seen it, I agreed.

"There are, however," Homestead added, "outbuildings belonging to the Bellassis operation, hangars and storage sheds that are not shown on this map. We have not been able to locate Mr. Bellassis, but since his wife is co-owner of the business, I assume her verbal permission will suffice."

Almost *wasn't* the co-owner, I thought, remembering the documents Park had had her sign before the notary that afternoon. Thank God she'd had the presence of mind to alter her signature.

Homestead said to me, "I understand Mr. Ripinsky is a well-known hostage negotiator, and of course my people are expert at controlling situations on the field, but it does seem a risk to involve you."

"My half brother is mentally disturbed," I said. "He often acts out violently in the presence of strangers, particularly strangers whom he perceives as intent on restraining or harming him. Aside from my mother, who lives in Boise, Idaho, I'm probably the only person who's capable of reaching him."

"Still, there are insurance factors, liability—"

"I'll sign any kind of waiver you require."

"Such a waiver would need to be drawn up by our attorneys, and I doubt they would be appreciative of being woken at nearly three in the morning. To say nothing of the tenants of the hangars, to whom we would owe courtesy calls before we enter them."

He'd pushed too many of my buttons. I said, "This is a man's *life* we're talking about here, not a few people losing sleep! Check with the law enforcement agencies that have jurisdiction over the airport—I'm sure they'll be willing to invoke probable cause."

Homestead sighed and rubbed a hand over his weary-looking eyes. "You have a point, Ms. McCone—several points," he said, and picked up the phone.

Another dark blue–uniformed woman on the customer service desk at the FBO welcomed Homestead warmly. "I received the call from your office and verified with Mrs. Bellassis that it's okay to enter any and all of the hangars and storage facilities." She frowned. "Mrs. Bellassis sounded upset. It's none of my business, but I'm concerned: has something happened to Mr. Bellassis?"

"Not that we know of."

"Well, that's a relief. He and his passenger flew out of here in such a rush earlier that one of the mechanics said he didn't preflight his Citation properly."

Under FAA rulings—and the rules of common sense—it's the pilot's duty, be he the first officer on a heavy jet or the owner of an ultralight homebuilt, to perform a complete preflight inspection. No one else, not even a head mechanic, can do it for him.

I said, "Who was his passenger?"

"A woman. I didn't get a good look at her."

I said, "Flight plan?"

"None, unless he filed it after he was airborne."

"Will you check to see if he did, please?"

She turned to her computer. "No, I don't see any."

That in itself didn't mean anything. Flight plans aren't required in many situations. And if Park had gone to their Napa Valley house as Lucy presumed, he wouldn't have bothered.

I asked, "How many people do you have on duty here tonight?"

"The mechanic I mentioned. One lineman on the gas pumps. There's a guy who's based at our Salt Lake operation sleeping in the lounge; he's waiting to pick up a pair of clients. Me."

"No janitors? No clients who rent hangars or tie-downs?"

"No. Although I did notice a vehicle driving toward the hangars at the northwest end of the field, but I didn't see which one it went to."

"What time was that?"

"A little before or after midnight. Rolf—the pilot from Utah—arrived a few minutes later, and we chatted over coffee for a while, so I suppose the vehicle might've left during that time period. But I haven't seen any activity on this part of the field since the We Deliver cargo flight arrived at three-fifty."

I looked at the clocks posted on the wall behind the desk: San Francisco, Denver, Chicago, New York, London, Berlin, Tokyo, and Wasilla, Alaska. Well, somebody here had a sense of humor.

It was 4:23. Civil twilight wasn't for at least another two hours; the sun wouldn't rise till almost six. That still didn't give us much time to work in total darkness—the preferable situation. I said to Homestead, "We'd better get started on those hangars."

Cargo flights from around the world were arriving sporadically now: FedEx, DHL, Lufthansa. They rumbled overhead on their way to the freight terminals. Traffic had picked up on the nearby Bayshore Freeway—mainly trucks, but some early commuters and travelers. The growl of the airport security vans blended in as we moved toward the cluster of hangars.

I sat tense and watchful in the front passenger seat next to Dave Homestead. Hy, in the backseat, was mainly on the phone, tending to RI business—a crisis developing in El Salvador, a death threat against a high official in the German government, an RI operative shot but not killed on a surveillance in Indonesia. In between he put the phone on speaker so we could communicate with Zoe Wasler, the operative he'd passed the tracking device to in San Jose.

She said, "We're about ten miles south of Fresno now. This person drives fast and has a nose for the highway patrol."

I said, "Where d'you think he's heading?"

"The way I see it, he's got several options: to Bakersfield and down to the LA area and get lost there or keep going into Mexico; cut over from Bakersfield into Nevada."

"He'll never get across the Mexican border," Hy said. "We've given the description of the car to customs."

"He could switch the car for another on some small-town dealer's lot," Wasler said, "but if he does that, I'll be right on his ass, along with the local cops."

"What about an airport or private field? Or a hiding place in the hills? There's that route—I forget which—from Bakersfield to Barstow that runs through some pretty desolate territory."

"I know the road. Besides, ain't nobody can hide long from ole Zoe."

This was a woman I liked even before meeting her. After she broke the connection I asked Hy, "Wherever did you find her?"

"She found us. Was with the Secret Service during the Clinton administration and met some of our people on one of his visits to the city."

By now we'd reached the first of the hangars. Homestead braked, shut the van's engine down. As we approached I gripped my .357. Homestead banged on the side door, called out, then unlocked it and switched on the inside lights. They revealed a midsize Gulfstream jet and orderly shelves covered with maintenance gear.

"Janna and Frank Favor's plane," he said. "They couldn't possibly be involved in this."

I knew their names. The Favors were well known in both aviation and philanthropic circles.

Next hangar: a perfectly restored and maintained blue Citabria like the one Hy used to own, until a crazy woman who had once tried to steal my identity had crashed it in the hills above Point Arena.

"Don Krall specializes in vintage restoration," Homestead told us. "He'd never risk one of his aircraft."

The plane was an absolute treasure. Hy and I nodded in agreement with Homestead.

Another FedEx flight was incoming. It roared over us, its lights brilliant splashes on the darkness, and I shouted to Hy, "If I don't get out of here soon, I'll need a Miracle-Ear!"

"Hah?" he yelled, mimicking deafness.

The incoming flight had diverted my attention to a structure close to runway 10L. I tugged on Homestead's sleeve. "What's that?"

He glanced up from fingering his ring of hangar keys.

"Storage shed belonging to Bellassis. It hasn't been used in years."

Hy and I exchanged glances, then ran together toward the shed.


One more incoming cargo carrier made the air around us shudder, the ground feel as if it were liquefying. I grabbed for Hy's arm and he clutched me tightly.

"Christ," he said, "I feel like I'm back in a war zone."

"Different enemy."

"Somebody does shit like this to innocent people, and they're all the same enemy to me. I don't discriminate when it comes to evil."

Neither did I.

The shed stood well out of harm's way, but it looked vulnerable. I shifted my gaze to the northwest, saw the lights of more incoming traffic.

"If Darcy's in there," I said, "we've got to get him out ASAP."

"Yeah." Hy pressed forward, pulling me along. When we reached the shed I heard noises coming from inside. Sounded like terrified wails.

"He's in there, all right," I said.

I examined the door; it was padlocked and the hasp looked sturdy. But its hinges were rusted, screws protruding. I indicated them to Hy, and slowly we began removing them with the aid of my Swiss Army knife. Finally they gave way and the door creaked open.

Darcy was curled on the concrete floor, arms behind him, legs bound at the ankles. He was shuddering, and when we tried to pull him up, he screamed.

*"No! Don't touch me! Nobody can ever touch me again!"*

"Darce, it's me, Shar. Please get up!"

The roar of the incoming plane was louder now.

Darcy cried out again and curled into a fetal position.

Hy had moved over to a far corner of the shed, drawn by a red light blinking on some sort of box. I hadn't noticed it until he swung around and said urgently, "McCone!"

"What is that?"

"Explosive device, armed! We've got to get out of here!"

"Christ!"

Frantically we took hold of Darcy's arms and dragged him out of there. He wiggled and grunted in protest, but we didn't let go. Twenty yards from the shed. Thirty yards. Forty, fifty...

"Get down!" Hy shouted. "Now!"

We both dropped face-forward, our bodies shielding Darcy's, our combined weight holding him in place. In the next second there was a booming roar and the shed blew up.

The concussion was powerful enough to shake the ground, the reflected glare blinding as the fireball blossomed into the sky. The heat was intense, searing my skin and hair; I heard the leather of Hy's old flight jacket snap and bubble. And then the echoes of the explosion faded and there was only the crackling of flames to break the deadly silence that follows a disaster.

I lay there shaking, the thought sharp in my mind that if we'd been two minutes slower in getting to the shed all three of us would have been inside when the explosive device detonated. Two short minutes, one hundred and twenty seconds—the thin margin between life and death.

The silence was ended with the drone of another incoming plane, and with shouts and sirens and rumbling engines. And Darcy sobbing and shrieking.

*"Stop touching me! Don't ever touch me again!"*

I freed my right hand from the tangle of our bodies, got a grip on Darcy's neck and put pressure on his carotid artery. It stopped his struggles and he lost consciousness.

Hy rolled off us, lifted me, and cradled my body against his chest. We both smelled of smoke and scorched flesh and hair. Our hearts were beating fast, but after a while they slowed and as we clung together while chaos surged around us, I felt myself slipping into the twilight state that gives the temporary—and largely false—illusion of peace.

Darcy was taken by medevac helicopter to San Francisco General Hospital, whose trauma unit is considered the best in the Bay Area. As the paramedics lifted him onto the gurney, he grasped my hands and wouldn't let go, so I rode along. When we got to the landing pad and the chopper crew tried to offload Darcy, he still clung to me with icy, rigid fingers. The ER personnel had to give him a shot of something before he relaxed and let go.

By then my hands hurt like hell, and I felt bruises and abrasions all over my body. I declined any medical help until they had Darcy stabilized, remembering all too well from personal experience how minutes—even seconds—can be critical to maintaining a life.

While they worked on Darcy I called Hy's cell: his injuries were superficial and had already been treated. He was now in conference at the Bellassis FBO with various airport officials.

A while later, after having my wounds cleaned, ointments and bandages applied, and a large amount of something—antibiotics, I presumed—pumped into my butt, I caught a ride back to the airport with one of the paramedics. There I located Hy in the conference room at the FBO with airport security, FAA people, uniformed police officers and sheriff's deputies, and a couple of men whom I identified from their immaculate appearances as FBI.

Homeland Security personnel were going to be pissed because they'd obviously not been informed early enough to get in on the beginning of this latest mess.

Oh, yes, there was going to be a jolly little jurisdictional squabble over authority on this one. I wished such nonsense still amused me, but lately the inefficiency and waste it created just enraged me and made me sad. Nobody won, and after the chaos it created few people were punished.

Hy's eyebrows and mustache were singed, his eyes tired. On the way in I'd spotted his beloved old flight jacket stuffed into a trash receptacle. I suspected that— in spite of the paramedics' ministrations—I didn't look much better, but Hy's eyes brightened when he saw me, and he excused himself from the circle of officialdom and came over to hold me.

"How's Darcy?" he asked.

"Physically okay, psychologically bad." I paused. "He's had a major breakdown. I've got to call Saskia and Robin."

"And I've got to get back to the aviation inquisitors." He jerked his thumb at the lounge. "Meet you here later."

I called Saskia: she'd heard the story on the early news and had already chartered a flight to San Francisco from Boise. She'd take a taxi directly to the hospital.

Robbie called me: maybe there was something we could do for Darcy after all, she said. She'd been overly harsh on him in the past. We'd see, I told her.

Ma, Patsy, and Charlene called: I was to let them know if there was any way they could help. My brother John called: "You go, girl. And why the hell did Ma send me pink bunny slippers?"

Elwood's message, which I accessed from my home machine—he distrusted cellular phones—said, "Daughter, I am here for you if and when you need me." Hearing the kind voice of the father I barely knew made me cry.

I spent some time with the aviation inquisitors, as Hy had called them. They were reasonably gentle and pleasant, as well as generous with information. They told me that the Citation belonging to Bellassis Aviation that

Park had left in earlier that day had been located at Napa Airport.

Zoe Wasler phoned Hy to report that the red Honda had cut over into Nevada, apparently headed toward Las Vegas. He told her the FBI was now on the case, and she should find a motel and get some sleep. Zoe laughed and said, "Not when I'm this close to Vegas. I'm gonna risk the overtime you're paying me at the tables."

Mick called. At first he sounded upset because he hadn't been able to help more actively on the case, then he slipped into melancholy tones: Alison had told him that she couldn't deal with a partner who practiced such a dangerous profession. He'd have to choose between her or his job.

"Which d'you think it'll be?" I asked, already knowing the answer.

"I've already decided. I love her, but not as much as my work. And I don't like being given ultimatums."

"Me either."

Rae and Ricky called, their voices competing on separate extensions. I should come to their place to rest up: Mrs. Wellcome wanted to feed me poached eggs on toast; Rae would read her manuscript to me and that would be sure to put me to sleep; if it didn't work Ricky would make me a couple of his world-famous martinis. Hy could come too, plus Alex and Jessie.

I declined for the cats, said maybe for Hy and me. Such pampering did sound tempting.

But first I had to sort out everything that had contributed to this sorry mess, and that wasn't going to be easy.

Not by a long shot.

# TUESDAY, SEPTEMBER 28

# Sharon McCone

And sorting it out sure as hell hasn't been easy.

Torrey Grant was taken into custody by the Highway Patrol heading east on Highway 80. Later she made a full confession. As Inspector Fast summarized it to me, Laura had confided the whole story of her relationship with Gaby and the alleged sex tapes while they were in jail together, on Torrey's promise to supply her with drugs when she was released. But Laura wouldn't reveal the whereabouts of the tapes. Or the name of the man who had molested Gaby. Torrey got that information from her sister, and then she and Morgan hatched their first plan: get hold of the tapes, blackmail Clarence Drew, and use the money to finance a drug deal.

After Laura was released, Torrey hooked up with her and Darcy and supplied them with cocaine. But Laura overestimated her capacity after two months in jail and overdosed before Torrey could get any more information out of her. That left her with Darcy, who she believed knew where the tapes were.

But Darcy was strung out and acting weirdly, babbling about a palace and Gaby being dead and buried in some cemetery under a coral tree. Torrey thought he or Laura might've hidden the tapes in or around Gaby's grave, and when that turned out not to be the case she'd taken him to the building where she and Morgan shared a flat, locked him up in the downstairs apartment, and kept him drugged while she tried to pump him for information.

When they couldn't get anything out of Darcy they'd figured Laura might also have confided in Chuck Bosworth, and Morgan had gone to see him. He'd beaten the Nobody when Chuck refused to talk, then shot him when he tried to run away.

Clarence Drew's suicide put an end to the blackmail scheme. So then they tried to extort money from Jack Tullock. And when that didn't work they decided to get rid of Darcy and bury his body in McLaren Park. The fight with Mick changed Morgan's mind, and next they came up with the idea of the ransom demand. One stupid plan after another. A comedy of errors, except that none of it was even the slightest bit funny.

Jeff Morgan was picked up by the FBI in Las Vegas and charged with kidnapping. He still had the briefcase containing the fifty thousand dollars on the seat beside him. At first he lawyered up and refused to talk, but when he was told Torrey had confessed he admitted to everything, including rigging the explosive device at the FBO—he'd been in the service in Afghanistan and trained in the use of explosives. He offered to cut a deal for testifying against Torrey. They didn't take him up on it.

Park Bellassis rushed back to the FBO from Napa and did a lot of hand-wringing about Torrey and Morgan. I was amused to read in the business section of the *Chron* two days later that Bellassis Aviation had gone into Chapter 11—something that had apparently been coming for a long time—and federal regulators were considering charging it with a number of violations of FAA rulings.

Park tried to patch things up with Lucy, but in a confessional and alcohol-glazed mood admitted that he was in love with a wealthy woman from the Napa Valley and had planned to divorce Lucy and marry her once he gained access to their joint assets. Lucy immediately had him removed from the house by a security guard she'd hired.

"He was all, 'We can try again, baby,'" she told me. "Can you imagine how immensely stupid he must be to've told me about that woman and his plans? And how immensely stupid he must think I am to agree to take him back?"

Lucy was growing up fast. While Park licked his wounds in the Napa Valley, she filed for divorce, put the house on the market, and placed the other assets in the hands of her father's investment advisor.

"Where will you go?" I asked her.

"Not far, maybe someplace on Lake Street. I like this neighborhood but—God!" She looked around, shivering. "It's been like living in a mausoleum. Part of Park's image thing, you know." She paused. "About Gaby—she was really killed by Clarence Drew?"

"Yes. Glenn Solomon urged the authorities to review the case, and they found overlooked—or suppressed—DNA evidence in the file that points solidly to Drew."

"What kind of evidence?"

"That he'd been with her the day she died. His wife, out of sentimentality, never changed anything in Gaby's room—including the sheets. And after she died, Drew didn't bother with the room either."

Lucy was silent for a few moments, her gaze inward. "And the sex tapes Drew made of him and Gaby?"

"You know, I doubt they ever existed. Jack Tullock swore they were a fiction Gaby had created in order to get the other Four Musketeers to kill Clarence. There was no evidence in Drew's house to indicate anything had ever been clandestinely taped there. No tapes have appeared on porn channels or on the Internet, so it's not likely anyone else got his hands on them. The irony is that if they don't exist, Torrey's and Jeff's plan was folly from the beginning."

"But that makes Gaby a terrible person—someone I didn't really know."

"No, it makes her a broken, desperate human being. She'd been victimized for years."

"But—murder?"

"Some victims see removal of the victimizer as their only choice. It's not an excuse, but an explanation."

Lucy nodded, but her faith in the friend she'd loved had been fractured. It would be a long time—if ever—before it mended.

"How's your brother?" Lucy asked.

"Doing better." Darcy was settling in at a psychiatric facility Saskia had chosen near Butte, Montana. A long distance from Boise, but she felt several degrees of separation were what both of them needed. She'd been enabling him far too long, she'd confessed.

Lucy sat in silence for a few minutes. We'd said everything that had needed to be said. I stood, held out my hand.

"Good luck, Lucy."

"Good luck to you too, Sharon."

Years from now investigators of unsolved mysteries will search for clues to the whereabouts of the Gaby Tapes and never find them. They simply don't exist. But people love to believe in urban legend, so the search for the tapes will persist until something hotter and more intriguing comes along.

I'm sitting here with a glass of champagne on our platform above the sea at Touchstone. Since we bought the place—for a dollar, but that's another story—Hy and I have always spent my birthday here. And the sunset is always spectacular.

That alone—in an area where fog often hovers and cruel winds whip the ocean to white foam—is a miracle.

Other miracles exist in my life.

I possess two dysfunctional families. (So far Elwood and the Malamutes remain a third, normal unit.) Yet in spite of their oddities—witness Ma's gift of the pink slippers that finally reached me and did indeed turn out to be fuzzy, bright-eyed little bunnies that I passed on for Lisa and Molly to fight over—I love them and they love me.

I have a strong marriage. Hy and I are in touch psychically, physically, and—thanks to what I consider the Instant Communication Age—by every cyber device so far invented by humankind.

Back in the city I can sit at my computer workstation in the soon-to-be-demolished Pier 24½ and instantly reach out to people in such diverse places as New York, Stockholm, Beijing, São Paulo, Cedar Rapids, Detroit, Calgary, and New Delhi. I can order almost any product I wish for and have it delivered to my home within a week (unless, as is often the case, it's on backorder). My news comes via the dying print media (I still prefer the *San Francisco Chronicle* and *The New York Times*), TV channels (although *not* FOX), and the Internet. Blogs satisfy my appetite for gossip, or occasional wisdom. I accessed the owner of the building near Pioneer Park where we're moving the agency at her home in Alabama and negotiated a great lease in one e-mail and two pleasurable phone exchanges.

But the miracle I cannot access is an understanding of the failings of the human heart and soul.

And so many whispers have haunted me during the long city nights:

*What did I do wrong, Darcy?*

*Why couldn't I help you enough?*

*Will you ever be okay?*

*Yes, you will. I've got to believe that because I've got to go on living in this world. And living a good life requires belief.*

*Not so complicated, if you think about it.*

Hy comes up behind me, puts his hand on my shoulder. It smells of alder chips; he's been smoking salmon on the grill. He raises his glass to me and then to the sunset. Says, "Happy birthday, McCone."

*Not so complicated at all.*

More mystery and suspense from

# MARCIA MULLER

Recipient of the
Private Eye Writers of America's
Lifetime Achievement Award

ೞ

Please turn the page
for a preview of

## *Looking for Yesterday.*

## LETTER TO SHARON McCONE FROM CAROLYN WARRICK, PROSPECTIVE CLIENT:

Dear Ms. McCone,

The world's forgotten me. No more mentions in the press. No requests for interviews. No photo ops. The websites are being taken down. I'm yesterday's news.

And I never got my message across.

Firearms. They should not—cannot—be allowed in the hands of the wrong persons.

I know the truth of that. Oh, yes, I know. I saw my four-year-old sister, Marissa, with the blood drained from her tiny face. Saw my nine-year-old brother, Rob, staring down in disbelief and horror at the gun he'd just accidentally fired.

And my best friend, Amelia, ripped and shattered by bullets on her living room floor.

When I was unjustly arrested for the crime, I thought I could make a difference. State my beliefs to the court and press, leave a legacy for all the countless victims of the indiscriminate sale of firearms.

Right from the beginning everything went wrong: People magazine didn't go into the issue, and adding *insult to injury, they used a bad picture of me—dirty hair and crow's-feet and snarly lines around my mouth.* Oprah *and all the other talk shows turned me down. I guess they didn't consider a woman who supposedly killed her best friend in a hideous manner and then was acquitted an entertaining draw.*

*Now I have my opportunity: Greta Goldstein wants to co-author a tell-all book with me, but Jill Starkey, that bitch who used to be with the* Chronicle *and covered my trial, is writing one of her own and trying to block ours. Starkey has attacked me in her columns from the first, and now she's bound and determined to profit from a false accounting of the crime I didn't commit.*

*Truth is, I feel cheated. I suffered all that pain, spent months in jail, endured that awful trial. I deserve to tell my story. Greta Goldstein's a best seller, and a profitable book would help me escape from my boring little job in the real estate agency; my tiny, damp, behind-the-garage studio apartment in the outer Sunset district; the defection of my friends and family members. I want to set the record straight about the loss of Amelia and Jake.*

*Always those losses.*

*Amelia, my best friend, and Jake, my former lover. She: shot multiple times by, as they now say, a person or persons unknown. He: believed the police's original case and couldn't bear to lay eyes on me. He's as good as dead, as far as I'm concerned. I bet that after I was acquitted, he couldn't bear to look at his face in the mirror, either. At least I hope so.*

*Am I bitter? Damned right I am. Am I going to do*

*something about this empty, empty existence? I hope so. I am requesting that you reinvestigate my case. I know this is unusual, since I was acquitted, but surely you understand how public opinion often overrides the judgment of a jury of one's peers. If you would grant me the opportunity of a meeting with you, I would be extremely grateful.*

*Yours sincerely,*
*Carolyn Warrick*

# TUESDAY, JANUARY 3

*10:00 a.m.*

Already I was tired. These boxes: how had I accumulated all that stuff during the years when my agency was located in the—now doomed—Pier 24½? Cardboard cartons filled the floor space in my new office on the top story of the narrow, blue house on Sly Lane, a short block above the Embarcadero, below Tel Hill and Coit Tower. I wanted to shove them down the chute to the incinerator and turn up the flames.

My office manager, Ted Smalley, had found the building shortly before the city's port commission had served notice on us to vacate the pier. I'd been dubious about the new location at first, but the underground parking garage and elevator—the old-fashioned kind with the metal grille—had seduced me. And the view was superb, even better than that from the pier, because I was looking out over the bay from a height of exactly 143 feet above sea level (a fact I wouldn't have known, except that Ted had been given a handheld altimeter for Christmas. It had become his constant companion so, as he put it, he would always know how high he was).

But all those attractions didn't hold a candle to the building's unsavory past—

My intercom buzzed. I picked up, and Ted said, "Your new client's here. Carolyn Warrick."

I had a new client? For an instant it didn't compute. Then I remembered her letter, which I'd received nearly a week ago. It had intrigued me and I'd researched her case, which had only intrigued me more.

I said, "Show her to the elevator, please. And warn her about the mess up here."

"Roger, wilco."

With the acquisition of the altimeter, Ted had become fond of using aviation terms.

I stood up, brushed dust off my jeans and sweater, and went to the elevator. It began whining and clunking its way up—noises that still alarmed me, even though the brand-new inspection certificate mounted on its wall said it was good to go.

When it arrived and settled—bumping some—I opened the grille. A woman peered out at me, her brow wrinkled and her mouth turned down. She was about my height, five foot six, with blond hair skinned back from a heart-shaped face and twisted into a bun at the nape of her neck. Better dressed than I, in a dark green suede jacket, black pants, and black boots.

"Ms. McCone?" she asked.

"Please, call me Sharon." I extended my hand to her, mostly to keep her from tripping, since the elevator hadn't quite aligned itself with the floor. "And you're Carolyn Warrick."

"Caro." She followed me into the office, glancing around at the stacks of cartons.

I invited her to sit down, motioning at the pair of clients' chairs.

"Sorry about this—we've just moved."

She selected a chair and sat. I took the other. There are some clients who feel more comfortable with you across the desk from them in a position of authority. Others want you beside them, to be their friend and—possibly—confessor. I sensed Caro Warrick was one of the latter.

"What a wonderful view," she said tonelessly.

"Thank you. When I get these cartons unpacked, I hope to enjoy it. Now, what can I do for you?"

She drew a deep breath. "Of course, you've read my letter."

"I did, and I've refreshed my memory of your case on the Internet."

"I'm surprised you agreed to see me."

"Why?"

"Well, the details are pretty sordid. Supposedly killing my best friend over a man, trashing her apartment after she was dead, trying to kill him after he found her body."

"You were acquitted. And you can't be taken to court again—double jeopardy."

"Acquitted, yes. But the stigma is still affecting my life. Many people have doubts about the justness of the verdict. As I explained in my letter, I haven't been able to get a decent job or afford a decent place to live. My family and friends have deserted me. Apparently everyone needs more proof of my innocence than the opinion of a jury of my peers."

"And you want me to supply that proof."

"As I said, so I can make it public in the book I'm co-authoring with Greta Goldstein. And I need it done quickly: a local journalist who has a vendetta against me is writing her own book and trying to block publication of mine."

"I know of Greta Goldstein's true-crime works. But who is the local journalist?"

"Jill Starkey." Her mouth twisted as if she'd bitten down on something sour.

"I see." Jill Starkey, a former ultraconservative columnist for the *Chronicle*, had covered Warrick's trial; her reportage had been negatively, even viciously, slanted. "Why do you say she has a vendetta against you?"

"I've always been a staunch supporter of gun control. For years I worked as an assistant director of the San Francisco Violence Prevention Center, and I had a close connection to IANSA—the International Action Network on Small Arms. Jill Starkey is a vocal member of the NRA. At my trial I spoke in my own defense, citing my beliefs and work as a reason why I couldn't have shot my friend. May I ask you something?"

"Go ahead."

"What is your stance on gun control?"

Not an easy question to answer. "I own two guns—for professional reasons only. I have a carry permit, but the weapons stay locked up most of the time. I take practice at the range very seriously."

"In short, you're for responsible gun ownership."

"Yes."

"I'm afraid I'm rabidly against firearms—with just cause. My father owned guns and kept one loaded in his bedside table drawer. That's where my nine-year-old brother found it before he accidentally shot my four-year-old sister to death."

God. That would make a believer out of anyone.

"Would my position prejudice you against working on my behalf?" Caro Warrick asked.

"No. I've worked for all kinds of people whose beliefs differed from mine. "

"In what ways?"

"Politically, religiously, racially—you name it. I learned something from each of them. All of them, I hope, made me a more understanding individual. Besides, our views on gun control aren't as far apart as they might seem to you. I'm for strict licensing. The need to demonstrate a reason for possessing a weapon. Background checks. Required practice; I'm a pilot, and I have to fly so many hours a month to remain current."

Warrick still looked skeptical. "Have you ever killed a person, Ms. McCone?"

"I don't see as it's relevant to your case."

"That's a yes, then."

"Okay, yes. In defense of myself and others. The nightmares still plague me."

She nodded, apparently satisfied with my reply. "Will you take me on as a client? Help me end my own personal nightmares?"

I considered. The woman fascinated me; so did the weapons issue. Also, I had too much time on my hands lately: my efficient staff had settled into our new offices and were proceeding with business as usual. Hy was traveling a lot between the various offices of the international executive protection firm he owned. Close friends were away on winter vacations. Hell, I hadn't even found a good book to read lately.

Instead of committing, I said, "Tell me your side of the story."

Three years ago last October, shortly before her twenty-sixth birthday, Warrick had discovered that her best friend, Amelia Bettencourt, was having an affair with her lover, Jake Green. She allegedly confronted Bettencourt at the latter's apartment on Nob Hill and, in the course of a violent argument, shot her twelve times. The crime scene, according to newspaper accounts, was chaotic—items of furniture and smaller objects smashed, walls sprayed with blood and other human matter, windows shattered by so many bullets that it indicated Warrick had reloaded her weapon—a nine-millimeter semiautomatic—and gone on venting her anger even after her friend was dead.

Jake Green was coming to pick up Amelia for a dinner date and heard the shots from the hallway. He rushed inside and discovered Amelia's body and was phoning 911 when someone stepped out of the shadows and fired on him. He dropped to the floor unhurt, and within seconds the intruder left the apartment.

Green immediately suspected Warrick was the killer— a suspicion he relayed to the investigating officers. They questioned her, and she claimed innocence, but two eye-witnesses said they'd seen her leaving Amelia's building earlier that evening. Bettencourt's family was prominent in city political circles, and Jake Green, an up-and-coming stockbroker with a large Montgomery Street firm, was intent on revenge. Caro Warrick was indicted and, in the spring, the case went to trial.

Warrick's attorney was Ned Springer, a public defender with a degree from what many considered a diploma mill in Idaho and less than two years of trial experience. No one expected he would win such an open-and-shut case, which was perhaps why the prosecution was not as prepared as they should have been. In the course of the trial, Springer stressed Warrick's staunch aversion to firearms and advocacy of gun control, and also brought a number of inconsistencies to light.

The murder weapon was never found, and according to state records, Warrick had never bought or owned a gun, nor was she the type of woman who would have known how to acquire a Saturday night special. The presence of Warrick's fingerprints in Bettencourt's apartment proved nothing, because Warrick often visited there. Warrick, a real estate saleswoman, had been showing a house in the Richmond district at a time that would have made it nearly impossible for her to have arrived at the Nob Hill building by the time of the murder. And no blood-spattered clothing or other evidence of the crime had turned up in her apartment in the Marina district. Plus Jake Green's obvious vengefulness worked against the prosecution.

Juries are notoriously unpredictable. Caro Warrick's had surprised many by exonerating her of her friend's murder. Now Caro wanted me to help exonerate her all over again.

I told her I'd think about it and get back to her within twenty-four hours. She asked about my fee and found it reasonable. After she left, I ignored the unpacked boxes and returned to my desk, swiveling to look out at the rain-soaked waterfront.

# VISIT US ONLINE AT

WWW.HACHETTEBOOKGROUP.COM

## FEATURES:

**OPENBOOK BROWSE AND
SEARCH EXCERPTS**

•

**AUDIOBOOK EXCERPTS AND PODCASTS**

•

**AUTHOR ARTICLES AND INTERVIEWS**

•

**BESTSELLER AND PUBLISHING
GROUP NEWS**

•

**SIGN UP FOR E-NEWSLETTERS**

•

**AUTHOR APPEARANCES AND TOUR
INFORMATION**

•

**SOCIAL MEDIA FEEDS AND WIDGETS**

•

**DOWNLOAD FREE APPS**

BOOKMARK HACHETTE BOOK GROUP
@ WWW.HACHETTEBOOKGROUP.COM